Maha Yogi: An Adventurous and Thrilling Story of Matsyendranath

santosh thorat

Published by santosh thorat, 2023.

This is a work of fiction. Similarities to real people, places, or events are entirely coincidental.

MAHA YOGI: AN ADVENTUROUS AND THRILLING STORY OF MATSYENDRANATH

First edition. June 2, 2023.

Copyright © 2023 santosh thorat.

ISBN: 979-8223316435

Written by santosh thorat.

I bow down to Shivshakti, and My all Gurus for making me able to contribute in Spiritual Literature.

Shree Ganeshay Namah !

Whenever Dharma (morality) falls prey to Adharma, (sin) inflates, Lord Vishnu incarnates in that era to protect the good and destroy the evil. With the help of many Gods , hermits and sages, the work of formulating a far reaching plan of religious doctrines and peoples safety is also undertaken. In the epoch of Lord Krishnas incarnation i.e. the end of Dwapaar Yuga, plans were made for the Kali Yuga.

Amongst which, was one of the most important plan; the nine Narayana's should take divine birth and educate the people to attain Moksha (salvation). On Lord Krishna's invitation, the nine Narayan ; Kavi, Hari, Antariksha, Prabuddha, Pippalaayan, Avirhotra, Drumil, Chamas and Karbhajan attended the Yadavas assembly.

There he told them the plan of who, when, where and how they will take birth. The incarnations were decided as follows, Kavi as Macchindra, Hari as Goraksha, Antariksha as Jalandhar, Prabuddha as Kanif, Pippalaayan as Charpati, Avirhotra as Naagnath, Drumil as Bhartari, Karbhajan as Gahini and Chamas as Revan. Shree Krishna as Gyanadev, Shankar as Nivrutti, Bramha as Sopaan, Yogmaya as Mukttabai, Uddhav as Naamdev, Maruti as Ramdas, Valmiki as Tulsidas, Jaambavaan as Narhari, Shukra as Kabir, Balram as Pundalik, Kubja as Janabai, and many such devotees and saints will educate people in Dharma (morality), Moksha (salvation), Bhakti (devotion), Gyan (knowledge), and Yoga; was decided as the grand plan for the future. Later the nine Narayanas stayed in the state of meditation on the Mandaraajchal. After a time interval, Lord Kavi originated in the chaste womb of a fish in the Yamuna River.

Coincidently, Lord Shankar was giving Goddess Parvati the teachings of self knowledge on the bank of river Yamuna. On hearing that, Kavi acknowledged from inside the fishs womb in the river. Lord Shankar immediately understood the meaning of it and blessed Kavi. Before leaving he also assured him teachings from Lord Datta in the future. Sometime passed and the fish laid eggs on the river bank. The egrets started breaking the eggs when a human larva fell from a big egg and started crying. He was the Kavi Narayana! Seeing that the egrets flew away and the child continued crying.There lived a fisherman named Kaamik along with his wife Sharadvata. They were a barren couple.

When he came to the river bank he saw this baby and got extremely happy. He thought to himself that this is Gods gift to me and took him home. The couple nurtured him with immense love and named him Macchindra. This child started growing up in the fishermen community and was everyones beloved.

From the age of 4 - 5 years he started going with his father Kaamik to the river bank. Every day the father caught fish and threw in the basket kept on the bank and the child protected it from crows and Soon the child got anxious due to the knowledge, he had received from Lord Shiva, when in the womb. He couldn't put up with the squirming of the fish outside water. Feeling pity for them, Macchindra threw the fish back in the river when his father was busy fishing. The fish got a gift of life. When Kaamik came back to the shore he shouted at Macchindra as his efforts had gone waste. "Child, whats the point in showing mercy on the fish You will starve! Kaamik dragged the child home. Macchindra felt,,,Begging is better than filling the belly at the cost of an animals life! as soon as the fisherman turned his back he ran away and day in day out kept walking towards North. He reached the Badrikaavan. Seeing the delightful place he thought, ,,this is the place where I should sit and meditate as per Lord Shankars advice. And that 5 year old child sat for meditation and ascetic practice!

Destroys all Ghost Tribulations.

THE POWER OF MACCHINDRAYOGA

It had been 12 years now that Macchindra was practicing asceticism. Lord Shankar and Lord Dattatreya came to Badrikaavan where they saw him. Lord Datta gave him divine vision and with love enquired about him. On introducing himself Macchindra prostrated before him. Lord Datta blessed him. He had weakened due to his ascetic practice which Lord Datta dispelled with the power of his blessings. He gave him Mantradiksha* and immediately Macchindra?s ignorance disappeared. He also asked him, "Where is Ishwara*? And Macchindra answered, "Ishwara is everywhere!" to which Lord Datta nodded in agreement. Lord Shankar also gave him divine vision and reminded him of how he had attained the Atma Dnyana* when in the womb of the fish. He told Lord Datta, "Give Macchindra the efficacy and power of Siddhis*."

Lord Datta asked all the Gods to grant him a boon. He guided him to gain victory over the Panchatatva*. He gave Macchindra, the Nath community, the name Macchindra, Shrungi*, Karnavedha* and other attributes along with the authority to conduct the Nath community. Macchindranath got the spiritual realization! And then they both left.

Macchindranath left Badrikaashram and headed towards the South. He came to Saptashrungi and started worshipping Goddess Amba. He felt like writing a scripture in poetic form which will be of use to people, but, which deity can give the poetic inspiration? He performed a Yajna* for seven days. The Goddess emerged in front of him and told him to attain Sabari Vidya* with rigorous Sadhana*. She took him to the Martanda Mountain. There was Naagasrvattha, the holy fig tree which had come to light due to the power of Nath?s Mantras*. On this tree were; Lord Sun and other Gods, fifty-two heroes, and twelve mother Goddesses.

The Goddess told Macchindranath to get water from the river on the Bramhagiri Mountain range and sprinkle it on the tree. She also cautioned him of the dangers in doing so. She said, "There are many small cisterns in the river bed. Take the Paandhari creeper and put one in every cistern. Have bath in the water from the cistern in which the creeper stays alive. Also fill the water from that cistern in a glass vessel and sprinkle that water on this tree. After bathing you will get a fainting fit but you should keep chanting the twelve names of Aditya which will help you stay alive and regain consciousness. Once you have sprinkled water, one God will be pleased with you. Again and again without getting tired you keep getting water and please the Gods."

Macchindra did as per the instructions of the Goddess. He filled the vessel with water from the cistern in which the creeper stayed fresh and bathed. Even though he suffered a fainting fit, he keenly kept chanting the twelve names of Aditya. That was when Lord Sun alerted him. Then he went to Martanda Mountain and sprinkled water on Naagasrvattha tree. This gave contentment to the Sun God and he promised Macchindra, "I will be present as soon as you think of me." This made him enthusiastic and he got water from hundred cisterns again and again and pleased the remaining God?s. All this took seven months. The deities gave him the required poetic inspiration. He wrote the Sabari Vidya* in poetic form. Macchindra was happy to have done something so enlightening! He took the blessings of Goddess Amba and left for globetrotting. He went to Greater Bengal in the eastern part of India. In a village while asking for alms, from inside a house there came a lady named Saraswati. He asked the seemingly unhappy lady the reason for her unhappiness. She told him of not having a child. On hearing this he felt sorry for her and gave her some holy ash. He said, "Mother, consume this holy ash and drink water. Pray to God! You will have a great sage named „Hari? as your son. I will come back after twelve years and take him along with me. Don?t forget!"

Macchindra left after blessing the woman. She told the entire scene to the women in her neighborhood. They scared her, saying, "This must be some kind of black magic, don? t consume the ash. You?ll turn into a bitch or something. Do not fall prey to these mystics." That woman got scared and threw the ash near the garbage place and heaved a sigh of relief. But indeed she had made a big mistake! Gods will is bizarre!

Fruition: The recitation of this chapter gives financial gains and success.

***Mantradiksha** - The initiation of mantras; **Siddhis**- The power of attainment of the supreme; **Ishwara** – God; **Atma Dnyana** – Self-realisation; **Panchatatva** - 5 elements of nature; **Shrungi** - Wearing ornaments made out of animal horns; **Karnavedha** - Hindu sacraments of ear piercing; **Yajna** - A Vedic ritual of sacrifice performed to please the Devas, or sometimes to the Supreme Spirit Brahman; **Sabari Vidya** - The knowledge of mantras for all round success and spiritual growth; **Sadhana** - Spiritual exercise by a Sadhu or a Sadhaka to attain moksha or a particular goal such as blessing from a deity; **Mantra** - An incantation with words of power.

MACCHINDRA AND HANUMAN

Macchindranath reached Rameshwar while doing pilgrimage on his route along the eastern coast line from Vanga Region*. He was about to take bath in the sea at Rameshwar when suddenly it started raining. A monkey started building a house with stone arrangement on the nearby cliff. He started wondering and said to the monkey, "It's already raining and now you will build a house? You don't understand anything!" That monkey was none other than Hanuman, the adorer of Ram, but in a small form. He said, "You seem to be a wise man! What is your name" he replied, "Jati, I mean, Yati*." The monkey said, "I just know of one Yati, Hanuman who is Lord Ram's attendant. I have milliequivalent strength of his. Let's see how much do you have!" Macchindra said, "You show your might At once the monkey took off and lifted a mountain. He threw it at Macchindra.

But he spell casted a weapon and turned it into ash which he threw in the sky and kept the mountain hanging. Maruti threw many mountains and Macchindra stopped all of them from falling on him. He chanted the Vaataakarshan Mantra* and splashed the sea water on Maruti. When Maruti became stifled his father Vayu emerged and along with him gave in to Macchindra. He promised Macchindra to receive full support from them anytime he wants. "While learning Sabari Vidya, Hanuman had helped me then why did he oppose now" asked Macchindra. Maruti (Hanuman) answered, "I was testing your capability!" There is a burden in my heart which only you can remove. Will you do me a favor?" When Macchindra agreed, Maruti said, "Years ago Ram, Sita and the monkey clan went to Ayodhya after killing Ravan.

Even I had gone with them that time. Mother Sita became extremely pleased on me due to my performance. She caught me in a promise that I should give up being a Bramhachari*, get married and accept to set up a household. I was stunned. I took this issue to Lord

Ram, on which he said, "Till date 98 Ram's and Ravan's have come into existence. I am the 99th one and even you are the 99th one. What will the wives of those devil's whom you have killed, do? You go to their kingdom and get married. Your whoop will be enough to get the women pregnant. And you will continue being a Bramhachari." "Lord Ram sent me. I stayed on the border of the women kingdom surrounded by mountains. My whoop made the women pregnant but they only delivered girls. Their queen is either Mainakini or Kilotalaa. She insisted on a physical intimacy with me. I told her, "Sage Kavi Narayana will later incarnate as Macchindranath, who will have the inheritance of an Uparichar Vasu. He will get married to you and fulfill your wish." I twisted her stubbornness this way. But the word that I gave her kept me anxious all the time. If you keep the word that I have given her, I will get rid of this tension.

Testing your might was just a way to gain your trust and so I challenged you. Can you please do this for me?" Maruti requested Macchindra. He got engrossed in thoughts. He was a sage beyond the fascinations of Maya* and Moksha. Doing as Hanuman expects will bide the establishment of India's future Nath community.

He had to accomplish his root vow at any cost. After thinking for a while Macchindra said, "Hanuman, Please don't put me in such a difficult situation. I don't desire to get intimate with a woman. You know the conditions through which Vishwamitra, Indra, Raavan, Naarad and also Lord Bramha and Lord Shankar had to go through, due to women! Then why are you putting emphasis on me Maruti was adamant! He wanted to accomplish the word given to Mainakini which was possible only if Macchindra agreed. Maruti said, "Mainakini will give birth to your son, Meenanath, who will also be an incarnation of Uparichar Vasu." Maruti predicted the future and kept insisting. So Macchindra replied, "First I will complete my pilgrimages and accomplish my vow. Only then will I go to the kingdom of women." Maruti said, "Okay! There is no male in that kingdom of women and if ever any male enters he will die. But I will make an arrangement for you to Macchindra promised Maruti and thinking about his vow he went on to make a pilgrimage around the globe.

Fruition: The recitation of this chapter will destroy the enemy and give knowledge to fight. Lord Hanuman's blessings will be within the house always.

***Vanga Region** – Greater Bengal, **Yati** – An ascetic, **Vaataakarshan Mantra** - A mantra to have control over the Air element,

Bramhachari– A celibate, Maya - Illusion

MACCHINDRA, BHAIRAV, MATRUKA AND GODDESS HINGALA

Macchindra during his journey decided to worship Goddess Hingala. That place was situated in a dense forest. Eight Bhairava's* were safeguarding one of the huge entry doors in the jungle. They accosted him. "I have come here to worship Goddess Hingala", said Macchindra. "We are guarding this place. You cannot enter without giving us a declaration of your sins and virtues", they said. "In my present state of renouncement, where even Yama and Lord Shankar, prove failures, there is no distinction between sin and virtue", he tried convincing them but to no vail. They rushed with big weapons towards him. Macchindra appealed to all God's and with a charm casted holy ash hardened his own body like steel. He challenged the Bhairava's and so they threw dangerous weapons at him but all turned out to be blunt.

He countered every weapon and proved the Bhairava's a failure. When he chanted the Vaataakarshan mantra and threw the holy ash, all Bhairava's fell down This defeat was reported to Goddess Hingala by five – six Matruka's*. The Goddess sent the Matruka's with the order, "Allure that Bramhachari!" But Macchindra was very cautious. Macchindra turned them crazy using the Kaamastra* from far away. All the Matruka's started laughing and dancing in front of him. Then he threw the Vaatastra* and their clothes flew away. They continued dancing unclothed. To humiliate them further he invented same number of young men in front of them and revived the Matruka's from the trance. As they regained consciousness, they saw the young men standing in front of them and ran away feeling ashamed of nudity. On their way back they saw the motionless Bhairava's fallen down on the ground. As soon as they reached the Goddess, she asked "What is the matter?" The Matruka's narrated the Nath's clout and Yoga efficacy and capitulated to the Goddess, saying, "He is the essence of eleven Rudra's*! You should also leave this place." Macchindra made the illusive men disappear and came following the Matruka's.

One of them saw him coming at a distance and shouted, "Look! First the Goddess with her conjuring power gave the Matruka's some clothes to wear and then saw who Macchindranath was with her clairvoyance. She saw the incarnated form of Kavi Narayan coming to her. On that she said to the Matruka's, "He is a great Saint. Don't be scared! Let's get blessed by his divine vision." Hearing that, they felt heartened. The moment Macchindranath came closer; getting extremely pleased, the Goddess emerged in front of him. He paid obeisance to the Goddess. She praised his valor. "Remove the charm you casted on the Bhairava's and get them back into consciousness! Child, I am very pleased by your feat!" said the Goddess. Macchindranath then freed them from his charm. The Bhairava's got up and started praising him. They said to the Goddess, "We were testing his supernatural powers when he defeated us!" The Goddess told Macchindra, "Child, we want to see your Yoga efficacy." He asked, "Mother, The Goddess said, "With your Yoga efficacy, keep this mountain in front of us, hanging in the sky. And later keep it back in its place."

Macchindra did as directed and while doing so not even a single tree or a stone was moved from its place. On this the Goddess said, "You subjugated the two opposite forms, air and mountain! You are a Sanctified Soul!" She gave him two new weapons; the Sparshastra* and the Bhinnaastra*. She made him stay and treated him cordially. On the third day she bid him adieu granting him a boon. The Bhairava's accompanied him and took his leave at the border of the jungle.

Fruition: The recitation of this chapter will bring to a person's life, freedom from the confines of deceitfulness, defeat of the enemy and accomplishment of all goals. He will become a respected courtier.

*__Bhairava__ - Guard God; __Matruka__ – Divine mothers; __Kaamastra__ – The seduction weapon; __Vaatastra__ - A weapon to control the air current; __Rudra__- A Rigvedic God of the storm, hunt, death, nature and the wind. It is also a name of Lord Shiva; __Sparshastra__ – The touch weapon; __Bhinnaastra__ - A combination of various weapons.

MACCHINDRA AND BHOOTPATI

Macchindra entered a dense forest named Bara Malhar. It was dark all around. He saw flambeaus moving here and there and immediately understood that those were ghosts. They might come to use later if he subjugated them, he thought. He formulated a plan and threw the Sparshastra which confined them to the ground. Actually the ghosts were going to the Vetala*.

The Vetala had sent some ghosts to find out why, among the eight crore ghosts only the ones from the Bara Malhar were absent. They saw that those ghosts were confined to the ground and even couldn't tell the reason for their immobilisation. The ghosts went around the forest in search of the reason and they saw Macchindra sitting in meditation. He was illuminated! They recognized that he is responsible for it and asked him, "Why have you tied up our fellow ghosts? Please free them! If we all do not go back to the Vetala, he will punish us. And he will punish you too!

Macchindra disagreed saying, "I am not scared of the Vetala! The ghosts started telling him the Vetala's efficacy. But he was not amongst the ones to get scared and put to flight the ghosts. When the Vetala came to know about it, he sent his battalion of ghosts..Macchindra was expecting that and so he created a crust around him by spell casting the holy ash. He chanted the Vajrastrajap*. Eight chief ghosts and eight crore ghosts came marching towards him. They attacked him with trees, stones and various weapons but none could cause him any hurt. All of it kept hanging in the sky above Nath. They bombarded him with fire! But Nath blew it off with the Parjanastra*. Then he created the Agniastra* and fled the ghosts away but they got back showering the sea water on it. Without delay Macchindra devised the Sparshastra and confined them on the ground. But the eight chiefs were not affected at all. They started troubling Nath With the help of Vajra mantra Nath protected himself and created eight Demons. Out of which seven

Demons fought a boisterous battle with the seven chief ghosts(Bhutpatis).

Seeing defeat the chief ghosts(Bhutpatis) disappeared. The eighth Bhutpati fell motionless due to the Vasavastra*. Macchindra used the Vaataakarshan weapon to drag the Bhutpati's together, to an extent that it suffocated them. That was when the Bhutpati's accepted their defeat and started begging for mercy. "If you leave us, we will do whatever work you tell us to do, but please save our life", groaned the Bhutpati's in gasps.Macchindranath said, "The poetic canon of Sabari Vidya that I have written already has the sanction of the Gods but to get that mantra into existence you must support me!" On accede; he freed them from the Vaataakarshan weapon. The Bhutpati's explained the rituals like worship ceremony, remedies, rosary, etc of the mantras and ensured him of getting quick results during eclipses. And also told what sacrifices should be made for the ghosts. All the eight crore Bhutpati's capitulated to Macchindra. Even the Vetala met him! They gave the devil his due! Everyone acclaimed the Nath Macchindra said, "The one who archives the story of our battle and reads it will never face a problem. You'll take an oath that even you will not trouble him or his family members and will protect them." Accordingly all the ghosts took an oath. All the ghosts and the Vetala bowed in front of Macchindranath and returned in situ. And this way Macchindra subjugated the Vetala and his accomplices.

Fruition: The recitation of this chapter will not allow anyone in the house to get affected by ghost tribulations. And if already possessed will help get rid of it.

*__Vetala__- A demon from Hindu mythology; Vajrastrajap - A chanting to attain the hardness of steel; **Parjanastra**- The rain weapon; Agniastra - The fire weapon; Vasavastra - An arrow of death.

MACCHINDRA AND KALIKA

During the journey Macchindra entered the Konkan region. He went to the Goddess Durga temple situated at the Adul village near Kudal. There was the idol of Goddess Kalika meaning a weapon named Kalika in the hand of Lord Shankar. He had used the power of this weapon to kill many demons and now he had given it some rest. That was the same Kalika idol* which was resting in the temple. She had acquired a no disturbance boon from Lord Macchindra worshipped the Goddess and invoked her, "Oh Goddess Kalika, please wake up. Bless my poetic canon on Sabari Vidya!" His act of invoking provoked the Goddess. She condemned him, "I never asked you to do the poetic composition. Why should I bless it? I am done with all my duties. Why are you dragging me into this new work? Get lost from here!"

Nath replied, "I am not leaving!" The Goddess warned, "You will also die like the small insects that pounce on fire unknowingly."

Nath said, "However tiny the sun seems, it lights up the entire world. You lend me your hand! The way Maruti did to the Pandavas." The Goddess disdained his superficial appearance and taunted him over his birth from a fish's womb. "Why are you begging? What is the use of the knowledge you have gained? You ran away from the fisherman's house! Won over the demons! Now what? You will subdue me?" Macchindra said, "Show me your valor! The leaf of a huge tree doesn't move without wind!" On this the Goddess Kalika got enraged and showed her flamboyant form. The entire earth was trembling in fear! The Gods were running here and there shouting, "Macchindra! Mind it! Commemorate your Guru! You have invoked the Goddess Kalika! Now you are left with no hope. There will be a holocaust all around!"

The Goddess bellowed, "You Mystic! I will grind coarsely along with you everything that comes in between the Earth and Sky."

But Nath didn't get scared; instead he threw a pinch of holy ash chanting the mantra of Vaasavaastra at the Goddess. The place got illuminated as if thousand suns had manifested at the same time. The supernatural powers of Kalika and Vaasvi* fought with each other in the sky. Kalika gulped the Vaasavaastra. He mustered the power of eleven Rudra's in a weapon but Kalika tranquilized the Rudra's with the help of the Mrityunjaya mantra*. Macchindra threw the Vajraastra* high up in the sky but, Kalika banged it on the Shailadri Mountain in the North due to which the mountain got compressed into half. That is why there are no mountains left beyond the Gurjar region (Gujarat). Macchindra secretly applied the Vaataakarshan mantra which affected Kalika and she fell unconsciously on the ground. The trees and mountains got crushed under her. She remembered Lord Shiva and invoked him saying, "Oh Umanath! Please rush to help me!" Lord Shankar understood that his powerful weapon, Kalika is in trouble. He immediately came there. Macchindra saw him and touched his feet. Lord Shankar held him close and appreciated him for winning over his weapon. Nath said, "Aadinath! It's your mercy! When in Badrikaavan, you made Dattaguru give me the knowledge and the power of attainment of the supreme."

Lord Shankar said, "Get Kalika back to her senses."

Nath requested, "For the success of the Sabari Vidya she should stay on my tongue and work as the power of the Mantra." "I will grant you your wish but first give her consciousness", said Lord Shankar. Macchindra took back his mantra and vivified her. She stood on her feet and greeted Lord Shankar. He said to her, "The way you have been my powerful weapon, henceforth you will be of help to Macchindranath and do a favor on the world." The Goddess replied, "I am your slave and will do as per your wish." "I will give you accomplishment in whichever Mantra you blend my name in", she told Macchindra. In this way Macchindranath acquired support of Goddess Kalika. Lord Shankar handed over his Kalika power to Macchindra and went back to Mount Kailasa. After that Macchindra headed towards the North direction of Konkan.

Fruition: The recitation of this chapter will beguile the enemy and he will turn naïve enough to be your friend. *

***Kalika idol** -A dark, black aspect of the mother-goddess whose consort is Shiva; **Vasavi shakti** -The magical dart weapon, unfailing at executing its target; **Mrityunjaya mantra** - An incantation to attain victory over death;

<u>**Vajraastra - The thunderbolt weapon MACCHINDRA, VEERBHADRA AND**</u>

VAJRESHWARI

Macchindra reached Hareshwar, a holy place situated in Northern Konkan. After having bath in the Gada Teertha* he circumambulated the mountain. He met the son of Lord Shiva, Veerbhadra in the form of a human being. Macchindra couldn?t recognize him even though he had the attributes; the Trishul*, Damaru*, etc. He saw Macchindra and asked, "Swami, who are you? Which cult do you belong to?" Macchindra answered, "My name is Macchindra and I belong to the Nath cult. I am an ascetic. I possess the various attributes; Shailee*, Shingy*, Kantha*, Zholi*, Mudra* and Karnavedha*." Veerbhadra disdained him. "You Sanctimonious prig! Mudra? Karnavedha? Who is your guru? Who has created this inopportune sect which is against our Vedas? He is a fool!" Macchindra got angry, "Why are you slandering? I am feeling like having a bathe again just by looking at you", hearing this Veerbhadra got enraged. He rigged his bow and arrow but Macchindra disdained him laughingly.

Veerbhadra also back answered him and got his bow and arrow in position. Macchindra charm casted the ash and created a crust around himself and countered Veerbhadra?s arrow by chanting the Vajramantra*.

Both the weapons banged on each other and got destroyed. They got into a dreadful war with each other. Macchindra countered the Kaalastra* used by Veerbhadra, with his power of Mula Maya*. Because of which the universe started assimilating.

The Gods asked Macchindra to take control over his weapons. The moment he controlled his weapons and used his Vaasanikastra*, the whole universe came up. Lord Brahma, Lord Vishnu and Lord Mahesh - the trinity manifested in front of Macchindra and introduced the both of them.

The trinity also created a bond of friendship between them. Veerbhadra was already impressed with Macchindra?s valour. He asked, "Macchindra what wish do you want me to grant?" He said, "To bestow a favor on mankind I have written a canon on the Sabari Vidya in poetic form. The person who chants the Shabari Mantra from it should get results." Veerbhadra agreed! The trinity gave Macchindra weapons; Lord Vishnu gave him Chakrastra*, Lord Shakar gave the Trishulastra* and Lord Bramha granted a boon of Amoghvaani*.

Lord Indra gave the Vajrastra, Lord Varun gave Jalaastra i.e. the efficacy to generate water from the earth. Every God gave him weapons as per their wish. Macchindra wanted to go to heaven and so the Gods took him along. He stayed there for a year. Later for seven years he stayed in various regions of the Heaven. The Gods bid him a farewell with love and he came back on Earth to continue his pilgrimage. In the Western Region of India is the holy place of Vajrabhagwati alias Vajreshwari.

He went there and worshiped the Goddess. There he was surprised to see hundreds of hot water cisterns. To please the Goddess he decided to generate one more hot water cistern. He asked the priest, "Who created these cisterns? When? And what is their history?" The priest answered,"Long ago Vashistha Rishi had performed a Yajna for twelve years. All the Goddesses had stayed here to attend the Yajna. They created these cisterns He looked for an elevated place and at that place he chanted the Jalaastra Mantra. A pit was developed with water in it. Then he chanted the Agni Mantra and discharged an arrow in it when the water inside turned hot. Then he had bath in that cistern and bathed Vajreshwari with water from the same cistern and worshipped her.

The Goddess got pleased and said, "I am pleased because you bathed me with the water from the cistern, you have created. You stay with me for at least a month now." With respect to her request Macchindra stayed there. He asked her "How did you get the name „Vajreshwari?" Goddess answered, "When Lord Indra came to attend the Yajna performed by Vashishta, not a single sage stood up to welcome him. He got angry and threw the Vajra on them. Lord Ram casted a spell on the Darbha* and with the help of his power made the Vajra incompetent. I emerged from that Darbha in the form of power and gulped the Vajra. Lord Indra surrendered to Lord Ram and so he returned the Vajra. Lord Ram enshrined me in an idol and bathed me with the water from the river nearby. This is how I came to be known as Vajrawati, Macchindra stayed there for a month and later headed towards North India.

Fruition: The recitation of this chapter will end mental agony and anxiety. Rebirth will be averted.

***Gada Teertha** - A mace shaped sacred pool; **Trishul** – Trident; **Damaru** – A small hourglass-shaped drum; **Shailee** – Mannerism; **Shingy** - A little blowing horn; **Kantha**- A loin cloth; **Zholi** – A square shaped bag made of red cloth; **Mudra** - Large rings; **Karnavedha** – A ceremony of piercing ears; **Kaalastra** – The death weapon; **Mula Maya** - The primordial energy; **Vaasanikastra** – The weapon of creation; **Chakrastra** – A serrated wheel; **Amoghvaani** - Infallible power of speech; **Darbha** – Also known as Kusha, the sacred grass.

MACCHINDRA, KING PAASHUPATH AND RAMACHANDRA

From there Macchindranath first went to Dwaarka and later to Ayodhya, where Lord Ram's descendant King Paashupath was ruling. Along with his huge army the King was at the temple of Lord Ram . He was worshipping Lord Rama. Macchindranath also came there at the same time. But since the King was inside the temple, the guards stopped him at the gate. "You Fool! Kaanphatya*! Move back!" Saying this they pushed him.

Macchindranath was angry not on the servants but on the egoistic King. He thought to himself, it's not right to punish the King as his populace is dependent on him. When the King was prostrating in front of the idol of Lord Ram, Macchindra used the Sparshaastra from outside the temple and confined him to the ground. Chaos spread around! People started talking, "A Yogi must have been insulted!" Some people had seen Macchindra being pushed. They started taking his name.

The ministers came imploring to Macchindra. The Nath felt pity and took back his Sparshaastra. The King got up and surrendered to Nath. As soon as the King came to know his name is Macchindranath, he took him to the palace and honored him. The King served him nicely and so Macchindranath got pleased with him, "King, tell me what wish do you have?" The King replied, "I desire to see Lord Ram of whose descendant I am." "Wow! What a great desire!" saying this Macchindra took the King to the huge open place outside his palace. And using the Vaatakarshan mantra he pulled Lord Sun along with his chariot on earth. The entire universe was set ablaze. Using the Jalaastra* Nath extinguished the fire. Arun*, horses of the chariot and Lord Sun fell unconscious.

The universe came to a standstill. Along with Lord Vishnu, Lord Brahma and Lord Shiva came to Nath and said, "Dear, why did you get Lord Sun to earth. See what a catastrophe it has proved!" Macchindra said to the Trinity, "This King Paashupath is a descendant of Lord Sun. Has he granted him a single wish till date?" Lord Vishnu said, "What do you wish? You first set free Lord Sun!" Macchindra said, "Lord Sun must prove an aid to the King always! He desires to obtain a divine vision of Lord Ram which Lord Sun should make happen. He should also make arrangements for the accomplishment of my Mantras.

Kindly grant the King his wish first only then will I free Lord Sun." And Lord Ram-Laxman manifested in front of the King! Lord Shankar rejoiced! The King felt blessed and bowed his head at the feet of Macchindranath and Lord RamLaxman. Nath prostrated before Lord Ram. He pulled him up and asked him his wish. Nath answered, "I should get your sanction for the mantras in the poetic canon of Sabari Vidya that I have written! But if you disagree get ready for a battle!" Lord Ram was highly impressed at Nath's heroism. He said to Nath, "The incarnation of Trinity is Lord Dattatreya and even I am alike. It's my duty to give you accomplishment in whichever Mantra you blend my name in. You are an incarnation of Kavi which means you are an inheritence of Lord Vishnu and even I am the incarnation of Lord Vishnu. So basically we are the same and hence the thought of a battle renders invalid. You made me manifest to my own descendant, which is indeed very virtuous. But why haven't you freed the base of our dynasty, Lord Sun?" Macchindranath pulled back his Vaatakarshan mantra.

Lord Sun got freed and started looking around. He felt like seeing the person who had tied him in the Mantra. The Gods told Nath about his wish. To not get affected by the Lord Sun's heat, Macchindra used the Chandrastra* and Parjanaastra* and he worshiped the Lord. When he got to know that Nath is an incarnation of Kavi, he also acclaimed a boon to accomplish his Mantras. After that all the Lords returned in situ. In the temple they performed a religious observance towards Lord Ram. Bidding adieu to the King, Macchindranath left for Greater Bengal.Fruition: The recitation of this chapter will put an end to all worries. And make a long distant friend come home.

***Kaanphatya** – One with split ears; Jalaastra – The water weapon; **Arun** – Lord Sun's charioteer; **Chandrastra** – The moon weapon.

MACCHINDRA, GORAKSHA AND GURU ADORATION

In Greater Bengal Macchindra was moving from one place to other soliciting alms. While doing so he reached the same village where he had given some ash to a lady named Saraswati. He went to her house. "Jay Allakh Niranjan*!" saying this asked for alms. When the lady came out he asked her name. "Long ago I had given you some holy ash, I hope you consumed it! You must have delivered a boy, so where is he? He must be twelve years old now," he said. The lady got scared and told him, "Due to fear I threw it near the garbage place. What should I do now? I have committed a sin!" Nath asked her to show the place where she had thrown the ash.

She showed him the place which was at one corner of the yard where there was a heap of garbage and cow dung. He remembered that the incarnation of Hari Narayana was going to happen from Goraksha – A birth in a labyrinth situation. The Nath called out, "Child! Goraksha! I am Macchindranath calling you out! You stayed under a heap of cow dung for twelve years, now come out." And a voice came from the heap, "O Great Guru, I am here! Pull me out!" Macchindranath said to the astonished lady, "Please get a spade immediately!" While the lady got it, people nearby had gathered around and were looking in wonderment. They helped the Nath in clearing the heap.

From under the heap came a twelve year old glorious Saraswati started crying cursing her misfortune. Nath consoled her, "What is the use of crying now? He is anyways not your son! Don't wait here or I might curse you." She went home crying. The onlookers were surprised and scared at the same time. Macchindra left the village taking Goraksha along. He initiated Goraksha into the world of Yoga and with a disposition of soliciting alms they started travelling to various villages.

Later they came to a village named Kanakgiri. Macchindra stayed back at a secluded place away from the locality and sent the child, Goraksha, to solicit alms in the village.Goraksha was a great adorer of his Guru. He rendered obedience to Macchindranath in every way possible. Even Nath loved him a lot. Goraksha went to the village to solicit alms. Inside a house the ritual of Pitru Shraaddha* was going on. Seeing a twelve year old boy asking for alms the lady in that house gave him Vadas along with various mouthwatering foods available in the house.

Goraksha got the required alms at one place, so he returned. They both ate the tasty food. Macchindranath felt like eating some more Vadas. He kept looking at Goraksha's face. He immediately understood that his Guru has something to say but is hesitating for some reason. He asked him coaxingly.Macchindra replied, "It would have been great if I could get some more Vadas."Goraksha said, "I will go back to that house and ask that lady. If she agrees, I will get some" and he left. On reaching the house, he called out, "Mother!" The lady came out and asked, "Now what?" "Mother, my Guru liked the Vadas a lot.Can you please give me some more alms?" said he. She said, "A great adorer that you are! I will give you more Vadas only if you give me what I want!" Goraksha said, "To render obedience to my Guru, I can give you anything." To test his words, she said, "Give me any one of your eye!" Goraksha immediately pulled out his eye with his nails and kept the bleeding eye at the lady's feet. "Mother, take my eye and give me the Vadas!" he said.

The lady got scared! And hurriedly got some Vadas and threw it in his Zholi. She said, "I don't want your eye. Now you please leave immediately!" She got scared that there will be an outrage in her house if her family comes to know of this incident. Goraksha gave the Vadas to Macchindra. His one eye was tied up with a cloth. When

Macchindra came to know the entire incident he hugged Goraksha with love.

The child's sacrifice for him, moved him deeply. With the help of Sanjeevani Mantra*, he retained Goraksha's eye. Macchindra got extremely pleased and gave his favorite disciple, Goraksha, the complete knowledge of Gurudatta Yoga* (a kind of yoga focusing on physical and mental strength building exercises and postures).

Fruition: The recitation of this chapter will help you get 14 different kinds of knowledge and 16 different kinds of arts.

*__Jay Allakh Niranjan__- Hail, the invisible power; **Pitru Shraaddha**- A ceremony to pay homage to a dead father; **Sanjeevani Mantra** – A life giving mantra; **Gurudatta Yoga** - A kind of yoga focusing on physical and mental strength building exercises and postures.

Fruition: The recitation of this chapter will help you get 14 different kinds of knowledge and 16 different kinds of arts and a friend settled abroad will come home.

GORAKSHA AND GAHININATH

Macchindra taught Goraksha Brahmavidya* along with all the weapons and various other Vidyas he possessed. He also taught him all the mantrasalong with the Sanjeevani Mantra. Goraksha memorized and exercised all themantras. Once in a village an unusual event occurred. Macchindranath had gone to solicit alms himself. A few children from the village were playing in a corner. Goraksha was also 12-14 years old and kept watching them play. The children came to him and asked him to make a clay bullock-cart.

He prepared clay bulls and a clay cart. Now they wanted him to make a cartdriver from clay. Goraksha prepared a small human shaped figure. At the same time just for revision purpose he was chanting the Sanjeevani Mantra. It resulted in the small clay cart-driver coming to life. A real child was created and started crying.

The children got scared and started running around shouting, "Ghost! Ghost! " On their way Macchindra met them. He reassured the children and took them back to that place. The kids showed him the clay cart from a distance and told him how the clay cart-driver got life. They also told him that a 12-14 year old Yogi had done this all.

Macchindra instantly understood that the children were talking about Goraksha. This was the consequence of the Sanjeevani Mantra! But Goraksha was not to be seen anywhere. Even he had ran away somewhere out of fear. Nath with his clairvoyance identified that he was Karbhaajan Rushi who had taken birth from that clay. He moved close, lifted the child and wiped his tears.

Macchindra along with the child went searching for Goraksha. He went to every house asking for Goraksha. The females got scared and the males accosted him. Macchindra answered, "A boy named Goraksha is my disciple. Let me first find him, then I will unravel the mystery." Listening to Macchindra's call, Goraksha came out from the place he was hiding. But as he saw the kid with Nath, he tried to run again. Macchindra caught hold of him and then kept the kid on a cloth. He assured him and tried understanding the truth behind the incident. "Karbhaajan Rushi has incarnated from that clay figure. Let's nurture this child and we will name him Gahini", Nath told Goraksha. He took them along and went to the place they were residing. He had decided to take motherly care of that kid but destiny had different plans.

The villagers found the Yoga power of Macchindra and Goraksha worthy of veneration but were not sure of their ability to nurture the kid. In the village lived a Brahmin named Madhu with his wife Gangubai, who was a very loving person. They were a barren couple. The villagers advised Macchindra to hand over the kid to this Brahmin couple to ensure proper upbringing. Macchindra did as advised and told the lady, "A Rishi named Karbhajan has incarnated with the inheritance of Vaishnavi*. His greatness is Gahan, meaning profound and so I have named him 'Gahini'.

Nurture him and after twelve years Goraksha will come here and initiate him into the world of Yoga. Gahini will be acknowledged as your child, but send him with Goraksha for the benefaction of the world when he will come to take him."

The lady said, "You are a Yogi! How are you so affectionate? Give me this child as my own!" Macchindra said, "Done! But don't forget, he will go along with Goraksha after twelve years." He handed over the kid to Madhu and Gangubai in front of everyone.

Macchindra stayed there along with Goraksha for few more days and later they went to Badrikaashram in the North. He wanted to keep Goraksha at Badrikaavan for Sadhana.

Fruition: The recitation of this chapter will help the females get rid of all the health problems. Children will survive. The mind will get rid of all duplicities. ***Brahmavidya** - A branch of scriptural knowledge derived primarily through a study of the Veda mantras & Upanishads; **Vaishnavi**- The sister of Lord Vishnu.

MACCHINDRA IN THE KINGDOM OF WOMEN & THE BIRTH OF JAALANDHAR

Macchindra and Goraksha came to Badrikaashram. Lord Shankar manifested in front of them when they prayed to him. He said, "The Vidyas you gave Goraksha will not be salutary unless Manojaya* and Tapashcharyaa* are practiced. He should stay here and undertake intense practice of asceticism." Macchindra asked Goraksha to stay there as told by Lord Shankar and left to make a Pilgrimage. Lord Shankar started giving personal guidance to Goraksha in Yoga Sadhana. While seeing various shrines, Macchindra reached Rameshwar after twelve years.

When he met Maruti after twenty-four years, he reminded Macchindra of his oath to go to the kingdom of women and marry Mainakini. Macchindra agreed! He stayed at Rameshwar for three days and left along with Maruti for the Kingdom of Women situated ahead of the Vanga Region.

Mainakini and the other women welcomed Maruti and Macchindra with great respect and joy. They gave them excellent thrones to sit. They got Macchindra introduced to themselves. Maruti said, "He is Macchindranath, the one I had said will come. He will complete your wish!" Mainakini fell for Macchindranath instantly. She freed Maruti from her demand and he returned to Rameshwar after staying there for three days. Macchindra got married to Mainakini. She gave him a splendid and happy life. In sometime, Mainakini conceived and at the right time delivered a baby boy. They named him 'Meenanath'! It was the birth of an Uparichara Vasu on earth. Mainakini pampered him a lot. Three years passed by happily. Meenanath grew extremely attached to Macchindra.

We will now leave Macchindranath here and will look into the life story of another Nath; Jaalandharnath. King Brahadravaa was ruling on the kingdom of Hastinapur. He was the seventh generation of Janamejaya*.

Two thousand years of Kali Yuga had passed. The King commenced the Somayaga*. Brahmins and Master of the Vedas were called from various regions. The solemnization went on for a year. God Agni was contented. Among the Navnarayanas, Antariksha Yogi took birth in the Agni from the altar. While removing the ash from the altar, an illuminated good looking child was found. In a surprised state the Brahmin gave the Child to the King. The King and the Queen Sulochana got very happy. The Queen said, "He is my second son!" Her first son was Meenaketh. They named this child, Jaalandhar and everyone admired him as he was the younger brother of the Prince. Jaalandhar started growing up. The King did his Munja* pompously. He also educated him. But when the King thought of getting him married, Jaalandhar was unaware of the concept of marriage. He asked the Queen. Whatever she told him was not enough for him to understand the concept. On asking how a wife is, the Queen said, "Exactly like me!" When he came to know about life after marriage from other servants he became reluctant and ran away without anyone knowing.

The King searched for him everywhere but to no vail. "A person born in such a divine way doesn't have the fear of anything. Don't you worry!" said the ministers, trying to console him in every way possible. But still the King continued feeling sad.

Jaalandhar on the other hand reached a dense forest. He was tired and so was resting in a valley with dense trees. A blaze of fire spread across the valley. All animal started running around; the burned trees fell down and even many animals died. There was only smoke in the sky. Jaalandhar was surrounded by burning trees. But when God Agni reached him he recognized, "He's my son! I had given him to King

Brahadravaa from the altar. He is the Antariksha Rishi!" God Agni took human form and woke him up. He stopped the blaze. Jaalandhar asked him, "Who are you?" God Agni answered, "I am Agni, your mother and your father! He narrated the incident to Jaalandhar.

Fruition: The recitation of this chapter will destroy the fear of fire. All problems related to child birth will be destroyed. *

Manojaya - - Self-conquest; Tapashcharyaa - Asceticism; Janamejaya - A King who conducted a great sacrifice for the well being of the human race; Somayaga - A sacrifice at which the juice of Soma is drunk; Munja – The thread ceremony.

JAALANDHAR AND KAANIF

Jaalandhar wanted to do generous benefactions for the mankind! When asked by God Agni he gave the same answer. God Agni took him to meet Lord Dattatreya. He welcomed them both. Agni said "Madan*, who was burned by Lord Shankar, subsisted within me. The child that I manifested in the Somayaga of King Brahadravaa, as a subtle illumination with the inheritance of Antariksha Rishi, is him, Jaalandhar.

The King nurtured him. He doesn't want to get married like all human beings. I have got him here to learn Aatmavidya* from you." Dattaguru asked Jaalandhar, "Are you willing to stay with me for twelve years? I will give you all the knowledge required." Jaalandhar agreed and stayed there. God Agni left. Lord Datta kept him in constant company. Bathing in River Ganga at dawn followed by Lord Vishweshwar's worship, soliciting alms in Kolhapur, repast at Panchaleshwari and rest at Mahurgadh, was their daily routine.

Twelve years later when he had acquired all the knowledge Lord Datta took him along to worship all Gods. All of them gave him various boons. He also summoned the Agni God and told him, "Your son has now become a learned and an accomplished Yogi. You can take him along!" but instead God Agni kept him in Badrikaavan for another twelve years to practice asceticism.

After those twelve years, Lord Brahma, Lord Vishnu, Lord Mahesh and also Badrinath declared him an ascetic. The son of God Agni, Jaalandhar had now become Jaalandharnath. God Agni was extremely happy! Badrinath addressed everyone, especially Jaalandharnath, "Prabuddha Narayana Rishi has already arrived into mankind. But do you know where he is?" Jaalandhar said, "Can you please tell us!" Badrinath answered, "Lord Brahma's Srujanshakti* sometime ago had come down to earth from heaven. At that time a giant Diggaj* was sleeping in the Himalayas and in his ears, fell this flash of light in which Prabuddha Narayana entered as a form of life.

He was in the form of a human baby. Someone has to remove him from the ear of that Diggaj. You do that work. And since he is going to come from an ear he will become famous as Kaanifnath. You give him knowledge and he will be your disciple.As asked by God Agni, Badrinath showed them the huge elephant moving around on the Himalayas. He was so dire that, if enraged would beimpossible for anyone to handle. Jaalandhar used the Mohanastra* and the Sparshastra on him from far away. So the elephant stood rooted at one spot.Then God Agni, Jaalandhar and Badrinath alias Lord Shankar went close to him and started calling out, "Kaanif! You are an inheritance of Narayana and son ofLord Brahma! You are the Prabuddha Narayana! Come out! Lord Shankar, God Agni and also Jaalandhar, the Antariksha Rishi, are calling you out. Your work is awaiting you! You can now manifest! Come out!" At that time a young ascetic peeped from the elephant's ear. He saw Lord Shiva, God Agni and Jaalandhar. He bowed and greeted them.

Then Jaalandhar pulled him down.

Lord Shankar and God Agni told Jaalandhar, "Giving him Mantradiksha* and knowledge is your work." Then Jaalandhar pronounced the Beejmantra* in his ears. At once Kaanifa's ignorance disappeared and the Ashta Satvik Bhava* developed in him. He had arevelation of Brahma Sakshatkara*. When everyone came back to Badrikashram, God Agni told Jaalandhar, "You should give him the knowledge and accomplishment that Lord Datta has given to you." And he took everyone's leave! Jaalandhar started sharing his knowledge with Kaanifa. Badrinath stayed there at his own will for six months and kept a conscious eye on his teachings.

He taught Kaanifa everything except the Sanjeevani Vidya and the Vaataakarshan Vidya, because he was not sure if Kaanif was prudent enough to use them the right way. On Lord Shankar's command he solicited all God's of Astravidya* from Heaven and Hades to grant Kaanif a boon. He also took a promise that, they will accomplish his mantra of Sabari Vidya. Then all God's went in situ. Hari, Har, Jaalandhar and Kaanif stayed in Badrikaashram for another four days.

Fruition: The recitation of this chapter will pull out the wrath of God's and curry favor from them.

*__Madan__ – The God of Love; Aatmavidya – The Metaphysical knowledge; Srujanshakti – The power of creativity; Diggaj A mythical elephant standing in one of the eight quarters of the sky and supporting the earth with the others; Mohanastra – The hypnotism weapon; Mantradiksha – The initiation of mantras; **Beejmantra** -The basic mantra, e.g. - OM; Ashta Satvik Bhava - The eight forms of spiritual ecstasies; Brahma **Sakshatkara** -God realization; Astravidya – The knowledge of weapons.

JAALANDHAR AND QUEEN MAINAVATI

Jaalandhar and Kaanif stayed in Badrikaashram for twelve years.Another twelve years Kaanif practiced asceticism on the bank of river Ganga. Then Jaalandhar left to make a pilgrimage. He survived on the money earned by selling bales of hay from village to village. He did not allow anyone to get a clue of his supernatural powers.

But God Agni asked God Vayu to suspend the bale of hay in air over his son; Jaalandhar's head to avoid pains to him. And that is how people came to know that he is some great Yogi. Still he lived in a filthy place outside the village. Something similar happened in the Helapattan town. He was walking with the bale of hay suspended over his head. The King of that town was Gopichand whose mother, Mainavati was a widow. She was a great adorer of God and a virtuous woman. A detached soul! But the King was absorbed in his luxuries.One day Queen Mainavati saw Jaalandhar passing by. She was marveled at the sight of a Yogi who was so luminous, composed and free from desire. She called her main maid and showed him to her.

The maid said, "He indeed looks like a great Saint! We should find out his where about." Mainavati permitted her to do so. Then the maid investigated and told the Queen, "He stays in an abandoned filthy place in very poor conditions. Such real Saints are sparse!" At night the Queen in a different attire and hidden face took her maid along to the place he stayed. Both of them went in front of him. They gave him obeisance and conferred on him cooked food and some fruits. But Jaalandhar abstained!

He didn't want an epithet! He threw big stones at both of them. He didn't even look at the food and fruits. Both of them sustained his throwing of stones and sat there adamantly. Jaalandhar saw their endurance and asked, "Who are you? Why have you come here at this time of the night? Why have you come to a fool like me?" Mainavati introduced herself and implored with ardor, saying, "I do not have any interest in being alive now. I want to achieve

Moksha, liberation from the bonds of worldly existence!" Jaalandhar replied, "You are the Royal mother! It will be such an ignominy for you and the king if anyone sees you here at such an hour. You please go back!" But Mainavati said, "I am going now! But will come here every night. Please allow me to be of service to Mainavati did not listen to him and kept going there every night along with her maid. She started being of service to him! She was an affectionate mother! This affection soon turned into devotion. As days passed Jaalandhar thought, "This old lady can actually follow the path of renunciation. It's been six months, but still she hasn't reached boredom. First I should test her tolerance! Only then will be the right time to give the Guru Mantra!" He then created an illusive black bee which started burrowing Mainavati's lap. Jaalandhar pretended to be asleep on her lap.

But intuitively he knew what was happening. Blood started oozing out from Mainavati's lap but she tolerated the pain keeping mum. She didn't even move a bit! Sometime later Jaalandhar pretended to wake up and with his mercy he cured the wound on her lap. He got extremely pleased on her!Mainavati's ordeal made him give her Yogadiksha* and Mantropdesh*.

The effect of which was such, that Mainavati got the realization of Advaitbrahma*. She went into Samadhi* but Jaalandhar got her back to Consciousness after some time. She became the disciple of the Jaalandharnath; a Saint, a Sadhu, Anubhutisampanna*, and a Nivrutta* Yogi! It is obvious for Sadhu's to think of the upliftment of mankind. So Mainavati also remembered her luxury absorbed son and thought that it would be great if her Guru uplifts Gopichand.

Fruition: The recitation of this chapter will rid you of the sins of killing a woman. *

Yogadiksha – To initiate into the knowledge of Yoga; Mantropdesh – The introduction of Mantras; **Advaitbrahma** - Indivisibility of the Self from the Whole; Samadhi – The conscious exit from the body;

Anubhutisampanna –A learned; Nivrutta – A renounced person.

GOPICHAND, LUMAVANTI AND JAALANDHAR

Mainavati was worried about Gopichand. She wished for his upliftment. She was upset with the fact of her son not realizing that his luxury absorbed life was perishable. One day the female servants were bathing Gopichand with essential oils, milk, honey etc in the porch of the palace. Mainavati was watching all this from the balcony. Seeing the King's intemperance's Mainavati felt sad, two tears dropped from her eyes and fell on Gopichand. The King jolted as he sensed hot tears. He saw up and seeing his mother cry he immediately went to her and asked "Mother, why are you crying? What has made you so sad?" Mainavati replied "Child, I cried for you. Your father was also as handsome as you are, but time swooped on him.

Today you are busy in your intemperance, but whatever you have is also going to remain here! Make your life meaningful by worshiping God." Gopichand asked, "But mother, where will I find a master who will give genuine Atman Dnyana and guide me towards the path of renunciation?" Mother answered, "A Yogi named Jaalandhar, of the Nath community has arrived on the outskirts of the city. You capitulate to him! Understanding wealth is perishable; you must concentrate on your upliftment." Gopichand said, "I shall take initiation after twelve years." On this his mother said, "Time waits for no one and so you should hurry up." Lumavanti, the King's principal wife heard their conversation. Gopichand was telling his mother that he will start preparing for the initiation.

She was shocked with the thought that the Queen will make her husband a Yogi like her. She called some of her friends, raised the matter in front of them and discussed the plan to deter the King from his decision. All the twentyeight wives of the King got together but no one could think of any plan. At last Lumavanti got an idea and she gestated it. After dinner, the King went to Lumavanti's palace. She attended him very well and pleased him. As the King got into a good mood, tactfully she took a promise from him that he would not get angry and asked "Is it true that mother-in-law has decided to take you to the saint Jaalandhar for initiation of Yoga?" The King replied, "Yes, at least so is in my mind." Then Lumavanti said, "May be you don't have an idea, but mother-in-law has a different intention.

She wants to expel you and make Jaalandhar the King. Hence she wants to turn you into a Yogi. There is no doubt that she will enjoy all the worldly pleasures with him. Once you leave God knows how miserable they will make our life. You must do something to cease this now." Listening to this Gopichand got furious. But he maintained his calmness. He did not speak a single word with Lumavanti and left the palace. He met his extremely faithful ministers in private and told them his plan. The same night everyone along with the King left from a secret route. Only a few heedful ministers knew the Kings where about. They found Jaalandhar and threw him in a nearby abandoned well. Besides which was a heap of horse dung, garbage and cow dung collected from the entire town. They threw that heap inside the well and buried Jaalandhar.

The King took a promise from the ministers to maintain confidentiality and returned to the palace at midnight. Next day everyone was passing by looking surprisingly at the well. "Who must have filled the ruined well with the heap of garbage? Anyways, good for us! Now there is no fear of anyone falling in the well. And that young Yogi, the one who roamed around with a bale of hay suspended over his head has left the village, it seems! No one can predict about these Yogi's whereabouts. But he was great!" People were passing by talking about him. All wives of the King were happy as they came to know about the missing Yogi. Mainavati lost hopes. The King pretended to be surprised. He had hidden from Lumavanti what he had done to Jaalandhar. Jaalandhar created the Vajrastra and Aakashastra* with the help of a Mantra and suspended the garbage in the air. He sat inside the well in the state of Samadhi. He didn't do anything against the King.

Fruition: The recitation of this chapter will free one from jail and that person will be able to live in society without any mockery.

***Aakashastra** – The sky weapon. GORAKSHA,

JAALANDHAR, KAANIF AND MACCHINDRA

Kaanif went to North after practicing asceticism for twelve years in Badrikaashram and Gorakshanath left in search of Macchindranath. But coincidentally Goraksha met Jaalandhar, the Guru of Kaanif, and Kaanif met Macchindra, the Guru of Goraksha. Goraksha went to the Helapattan village and enquired about Macchindra.

He came to know from the people that a Yogi named Jaalandhar had been there. They also told him how he was and how one day he had gone missing. Later while Goraksha was booming Allakh Niranjan he got a reciprocation from under the ground. He asked, "Who are you and where are you?" to which he got a reply, "I am Jaalandhar and am under the earth's surface." Goraksha said, "I am Goraksha, Macchindranath's disciple. But how do you stay under the surface?" Jaalandhar reported the Mainavati and Gopichand scene. "I will burn the King who did this to you", said Goraksha. Jaalandhar told him, "You don't do anything. My disciple Kaanif will meet you on the way.

He will do whatever he has to. Whatever is happening will increase the glory of our Nath community and even Gopichand will get redemption. Don't worry!" Goraksha agreed to it and he left for Jagannathpuri. On the other side Kaanifnath was making his pilgrimage. Due to his influence he made more than seven hundred disciples. He turned from North to East and crossing the Vanga region he reached the border of the Kingdom of Women. Lord Hanuman was the guardian of that border. He had come there from Rameshwar at the same time. Kaanifnath saw him. Lord Hanuman asked him not to enter the Kingdom of Women but he didn't listen and bound him with the help of Sparshastra. For some time Maruti rooted to the spot but got free due to the force of air. He thought to himself, if Kaanif meets Mainakini and Macchindra he might take Macchindra along.

So he should be frightened and made to return from here.Maruti expanded to the size of a mountain and seeing that the disciples started running away. But Kaanif stopped them and started battling with him. Maruti threw boulders and stones at them. Kaanif pulverized those with the Vajrastra. And when that Astra was about to hit, Maruti crushed it with a punch. Then Kaanif chanted the Mantra of Kalika, Agni, Indra and Vayu and threw all these weapons together. Due to which Maruti got rooted. He threw the Agniastra in the sea and requested the Vayuastra* that he doesn't want to get killed from his own father. Vayu told Maruti, "Kaanif is valorous like Macchindranath and you'll be helpless in front of him. So make him your friend instead." On the other hand, the sea water was boiling due to Agni and aquatic life had started dying.

The sea came there in human form and along with Vayu, introduced Kaanif and Maruti to each other. Kaanif said, "We want to go and come back from the Kingdom of Women, please don't stop us!" Maruti told him how Macchindra had freed him from the pledge, how he had agreed to marry Mainakini and how bad she will feel if he will be taken away from there. He also stipulated a condition, "Don't talk to Macchindra about the world of Yoga." After which Kaanif entered the Kingdom of Women. Macchindra came to know about the arrival of Kaanif. "Hope the great sage of our Nath community hasn't come here to take me away!" feared Macchindra. Even then along with Mainakini and Meenanath, he gave a grand welcome to Kaanif and his disciples.

He made them stay there for a month and served them extremely well in all possible ways. He realized that they had come with Lord Hanuman's permission and so were still alive in this Kingdom of Women. He also came to know about Jaalandharnath and Kaanifnath's birth and the knowledge they had acquired. He gave a lot of respect to Kaanif as he is the disciple of Lord Shankar and Lord Datta.

Fruition: The recitation of this chapter will end all fights in the house and will bring peace to the family.

*__Vayuastra__– The air weapon GORAKSHA,

KAANIF, GOPICHAND AND MAINAVATI

"If Kaanif leaves from here, he will tell Gorakshanath my where about and then he will take me from here. So it's better I keep Kaanif engrossed in pleasures for a month with the help of Mohajaal*," thought Macchindra and did accordingly. But to no vail. Kaanif left the Kingdom of Women along with his disciples. He became famous where ever he went. As he reached Goud Region*, the King Gopichand of Helapattan came to know of his valour. He sent his messenger to call Kaanif. Goraksha and Kaanif encountered each other at a jungle. They started talking to each other and examined each other's Siddhis*. With the power of their Siddhi's they got the mangoes from a distant tree, near to them.

But Kaanif did not have the Siddhi of putting the mangoes back on tree. Goraksha said, "Nothing is impossible for a real disciple of Guru". Kaanif told Goraksha how his Guru Macchindra has setup his household in the Kingdom of Women and mocked him. On that Goraksha got enraged and told him how King Gopichand has buried his Guru Jaalandhar under a heap of dung. Goraksha showed his superiority of Siddhi's by putting the mangoes back on the tree. On which Kaanif acknowledged his Superiority. This is how both of them came to know of their Guru's whereabouts. Kaanif went to meet Gopichand. "How great and glorious Kaanifnath is! He also has a great number of disciples! Such a Guru will suit me! And unlike him, Jaalandhar sat near the heap of garbage." thought Gopichand. Kaanif was furious but had decided not to react until he meets his Guru and gets to know what had really happened.

He accepted all the hospitality the King gave him, and when the King said, "It would be a blessing if you initiate me." Kaanif replied, "King, you want me to initiate you only because my glory has impressed you. But where did you send the great sage from whom you should have taken real initiation? You have buried him in dung and garbage! Why are you beseeching in front of me!" The king jolted! He didn't understand how Kaanif had come to know of something he had done very secretly. He started asking for forgiveness. Kaanif was a sage and so he said, "Don't worry, we will find out some solution for it!"

The news reached Mainavati and she got furious at the King. But he was extremely ashamed of his actions and asked for her forgiveness as well. When Mainavati told Kaanif that she is Jaalandhar's disciple, he said, "Then how did you give the permission to bury your Guru? Is this your devotion towards him?" Mainavati said, "I didn't know all this.

I had told my son to take initiation from him and he did all this without anyone knowing of it. What should I do now? If the Nath is alive his wrath will bring misery to us. You are like a brother to me as we have the same Guru. Please save us from all this!" and prayed to him helplessly. Kaanif melted and said, "Don't be scared! I will do something for the King's safety." Mainavati felt a bit relaxed. She told everything to Gopichand. Even he felt relaxed. The King didn't know if Jaalandhar was alive or not but Mainavati had a feeling that her Guru will surely be alive in the well in Samadhi state. **Fruition:** The recitation of this chapter will free one from nightmares.

***Mohajaal** – Snare of temptations; **Goud Region** – Region on the bank of River Godavari; **Siddhi** – The power of attainment of the supreme.

KAANIF, GOPICHAND AND JAALANDHAR

What an amazing trick he did! Kaanif asked the king to prepare five self statues all in different metals. They were ready in few days. Then Kaanif along with the King went to the place where Jaalandhar was buried. He told the King to keep one statue on the well and strike the hoe on the garbage heap. It was decided that the King will move aside after striking on the heap. When Jaalandhar will ask, "Who is digging?" he should give an answer, "It? s me, Gopichand." As he struck the hoe Jaalandhar asked the same question and the King answered as decided.

And instantly the statue got burnt due to Jaalandhar?s wrath. In the same way even the remaining statues got destroyed. Jaalandhar thought, "Gopichand has burnt. But now if I see him alive he will become Chiranjiv*!"Later Kaanif answered, "Respected Guru, I am Kaanif, your disciple. I have got Gopichand here." Hearing this Jaalandhar got excited to meet his disciple and his wrath subdued. "Gopichand, may you become a Chiranjiv!" blessed Jaalandhar.

He destroyed the Aakashastra and Vajrastra and came out of the well. He met Kaanif with love. When Gopichand held his feet crying in regret he said, "King you are alive today only because of Kaanif. You will become a Chiranjiv! Now you decide whether you want to stay holding the pleasures of your perishable youth, your Kingdom and your wealth or you want to walk the path of asceticism." Gopichand had come to know of Jaalandhar?s power of Yoga. "I am alive today only because of Nath?s mercy or else I would have been incinerated", thinking this he instantaneously decided to give up his worldly pleasures and take Nath?s grace.

He capitulated to Jaalandhar. Looking at his determination Jaalandhar looked at the King from head to toe. The King felt excitement throughout his body. Then Jaalandhar whispered the Guru

Mantra in his ears. And the King realized, „God is the ultimate truth and everything else is false?. Jaalandhar gave him the attire of a Yogi. His hair got matted. Where once there was combed hair now there was matted hair.

There came a Zholi on his shoulder. A pleasant face, manner and Shrungi! Gopichand who was the King now became an effigy of asceticism. He touched Jaalandhar?s feet and started dancing holding his hand! Jaalandhar put Gopichand in a critical situation. "Go to the palaw2qxsce and solicit alms from your own wives! Break their snare of affection, compassion and hopes." Saying this Kaanif and Jaalandhar sent the King to his palace. The King came to the palace to solicit alms. People gathered to see him.

The Queens were shattered and started crying. They surrounded him and requested to return. "At least stay in front of our eyes always! We will be of service to you!" said the Queens. To all that they said he just replied saying, "Allakh Niranjan!" Mainavati being a Sannyasini*, she gave alms to her son. Taking that the King came to Jaalandhar. Mainavati also followed him.

Jaalandhar taught Gopichand many important things from the Yoga Vidya. After 3-4 days he told Gopichand, "Now leave this town and go to Badrikaashram for practicing asceticism. Your practice should continue for twelve years. Mainavati will stay in the palace." Lumavanti was regretting very much and being a domestic married woman, Nath forgave her. Muktachand, the Prince was coroneted. The ministers and the loyal knights were honored. Nath stayed there for six months and managed Mainavati, Lumavanti and all the ministers.

Fruition: The recitation of this chapter will help attain Yoga Siddhi and one will become virtuous.

***Chiranjiv** – These are permanent lived beings in Hinduism who are to remain alive through this Kali Yuga until the next Satya Yuga; **Sannyasini** - A female renouncer. GOPICHAND,

CHAMPAVATI AND TILAKCHAND

On the way to Badrikaashram, Gopichand was accepting only alms and he reached a town named Paulapattan. His sister Champavati was the daughter-in-law of the King of that town. The news of Gopichand turning a Sannyasin* had already reached there. Her in-laws started mocking him. He being a Sannyasin was resting near a reservoir thinking why to go to Champavati's place.

But her female maids had already given the news. Her inlaws thought if the brother of our daughter-in-law solicits alms in our town, it will be shameful to our prestige. They sent him an insistent invitation with the maids to come to the palace on behalf of Champavati. Since the message was, "Don't break your sister's heart", he went to the palace. On reaching the palace they made him sit in the stable without allowing him to meet Champavati.

Even the food was served to him by servants, in the stable. But as per the ethos of asceticism, he started eating that acquired food without considering it as a dishonor. Meanwhile the maids secretly showed Champavati her brother and taunted her saying, "He's your brother, right? Why has he become a beggar? See how he is eating the acquired food voraciously!" along with many others things. Her sister-in-laws and the others also humiliated her.

That was when Champavati couldn't bear the sorrow and committed suicide when alone by stabbing her stomach with a dagger. The maids found her dead and lamentation spread all around. Some said, "Champavati died due to her brother's sorrow", others said, "This mystic entered the house and became a reason for her death!" The rumor spread and it also reached Gopichand in the stable. He felt, "I am responsible for Champavati's death and this will stay in everyone's mind". And so he felt grief even though he was an ascetic. He was helpless! Gopichand accompanied the people in Champavati's funeral cortege.

He was missing his Guru Jaalandharnath and thought to himself, "If he was here, he would have vivified Champavati." He started requesting people, "Please don't burn my sister's corpse! Just wait for some time! My Guru Jaalandharnath is a great Yogi! I will get him here from Helapattan. He will surely vivify my sister!" People made fool of him and abstained from listening. He got on top of her pyre and said, "Burn me also!" Finally Tilakchand said, "Cut Champavati's left hand and give it to him. Let him take it along! Let's see how great his Guru is!" He told Gopichand, "You come soon! We will not burn the corpse!" Gopichand left for Helapattan with a sorrowful heart with his sister's trimmed off hand.To avoid the turmoil due to Gopichand's arrival in the town, Jaalandharnath chanted the mantra of Prayanaastra* and hastily met him five miles on his way to town. Gopichand told him what had happened with his sister and how he had left from there after taking a vow of getting his sister vivified by his Guru.

Then Jaalandhar took him along and came down from sky in the crematorium at the speed of air where people were mourning. Tilakchand was shocked! He had not expected the Guru to be there so soon. "He seems to be a great sage!" saying this he ran towards Jaalandhar to touch his feet. But ignoring him, Jaalandhar held the corpse's hand and chanted the Sanjeevani Mantra.

He casted ash on the hand and said, "Champavati, get up and come here!" To everyone's surprise she got up from the pyre and came to Everyone acclaimed Jaalandhar! As he was leaving for Helapattan, Tilakchand started saying with too much respect, "Please do a favor on us! Everyone intends to have a meal with you. Please do not hesitate!" Jaalandhar agreed! He asked Champavati to prepare food and made her sit along with her husband to have food next to him.

He fed both of them a morsel from his own plate and gave them a blessing of immortality.

After that he left! He said to Tilakchand, "Gopichand is in Badrikaashram. His son has been crowned a King! You should protect him! Even I am going to stay here for a few months." A few years later, Jaalandhar went to Badrikaashram along with Kaanif. Gopichand was practicing asceticism for twelve years. Jaalandhar helped him complete his practice and called the God's of mantras to grant him a boon which made him an accomplished ascetic. **Fruition:** The recitation of this chapter will help get rid of Brahmahatyaa Dosha* and ancestors will be liberated from the Kumbhipakam Naraka*.

***Sannyasin**– A male renouncer; Prayanaastra – The departure weapon; **Brahmahatyaa Dosha** – It's a sin occurred due to killing of a Vedic Brahmin; **Kumbhipakam Naraka** – It is a hell that is mentioned in Hindu Tradition. This punishment is given to people who harm innocent living beings on earth.

GORAKSHA, MARUTI AND SHRI RAM

Goraksha came near the Kingdom of Women after a lot of travel. That time a dancer named Kalinga and a few other dancers were going to that Kingdom to earn money from dancing. Gorakshanath asked, "I am good at singing and playing musical instruments. Can I come along as a member of your team.?" The females examined his talent. When he started singing and playing the musical instruments casting ash, the trees and stones also started singing with him.

Seeing the miracle Kalinga decided to take him along. As per the rules of the Kingdom of Women he was not going to be able to enter in a man's attire. So they decided to take him along in a woman's attire and gave him a false name, Purvad Kalinga did all this as any man was to die if he entered the Kingdom of Women. She said, "Here women get pregnant due to Lord Hanuman's whoop." Goraksha said, "You'll , don't worry! My power of Yoga is much more than Hanuman. I am an ascetic! I don't want money, just food to eat twice a day!"

Goraksha had planted the Vajrastra, Mohanastra, Sparshastra and Naagastra* on the boundary. That night everyone stayed at the Chinnapattan village.

At night when Lord Hanuman came there the Vajrastra banged on him. When he fell down he got stuck to the ground due to Sparshastra. Due to Mohanastra he forgot the reason for which he was there. And due to Naagastra his hands and legs coiled which made him restless. Lord Hanuman invoked Lord Ram to get out of the mess.

To release his devotee, Lord Ram came there himself. He used the Indrastra*, Vishnuastra* and Garudastra* respectively to defend Vajrastra, Mohanastra and the Naagastra. He used the Vibhaktaastra* to free Maruti from the ground. Lord Ram came to know with his clairvoyance that Hari Narayana in the form of Goraksha has entered the Kingdom in a woman's attire and is staying in Chinnapattan village. On telling this to Lord Hanuman, he requested, "Now he might take Macchindra along! We should stop him. Please change his mind with your dulcet pledge!" Lord Ram decided to do accordingly.

Lord Ram and Lord Hanuman came to the place where Goraksha was residing in the form of learned Brahmins. He was engrossed in meditation and swaying happily to the commemoration of Macchindra. They both came in front of him. Firstly Lord Ram praised his qualities. Goraksha said, "I am a Yogi! Why are you praising me so much? What do you want me to do for you?" Lord Ram replied, "The work is not too big! I will tell you but you should do it! We are petitioner Brahmins! We have come to you with some expectations. You promise that you will do it!"

Goraksha started deducing in his mind. "In the Kingdom where male entry is banned, how come these Brahmins are trafficking without any fear at this hour of the night? This means they must be one of the Trinity(Lord Brahma ,Lord Vishnu ,Lord Shiva)! I have work with Macchindra. I can agree anything that is not related to him." He said, "Since you have come to the Kingdom where male entry is banned, you must be one of the Trinity! In that case what can a Yogi like me give you? What promise can I give?" and bowed in front of them in adoration.

That resulted in Lord Ram and Lord Hanuman revealing their actual self. They said, "Goraksha, Mainavati has asked for Macchindra as a parole from Lord Hanuman. You have come here, but should not take Macchindra along. This is Lord Hanuman's wish. Think about it!" Goraksha replied, "It is not right for a great, unique and generous sage to leave the work of upliftment and get attached to worldly pleasures.

I will take him along come what may!" Lord Hanuman got enraged but Lord Ram told them not to fight. Goraksha asked for forgiveness from Lord Ram for his act of trapping Lord Hanuman with the various

Astra's and Lord Ram had to come himself to save him. Lord Ram hugged him tightly and left!

Fruition: The recitation of this chapter will open all doors to attain Moksha.

***Naagastra** – The snake weapon; **Indrastra** – The weapon to shower arrows from the sky; **Vishnuastra** – The weapon to shower arrows and discs;

Garudastra - A celestial weapon used to defend against Naagastra; **Vibhaktaastra** – The separation weapon.weapon to shower arrows and discs; **Garudastra** - A celestial weapon used to defend against Naagastra;

THE MEETING OF GORAKSHANATH AND MACCHINDRANATH

Maruti met Mainakini and told her, "Gorakshanath, a disciple of Macchindra has come here to take him along and so you should dissuade your husband from him with love." He also said, "Macchindra got married to you and you also have a son. Now even he would not take delight in staying here, I think." Listening to that Mainakini felt scared of the future anguish of separation.(Flashback – Mainakini was born on Sinhala Island and her name was Padmini. Once she had laughed at an Uparichar Vasu travelling in the sky. She had got aroused looking at him. And the Uparichar Vasu had cursed her, "You will stay in the Kingdom of Women where you will not get to see any man." On asking him to take back his curse he said, "In that Kingdom is a Queen named Kilotala.

After her death you will be the Queen of that Kingdom. You should ask Lord Hanuman for physical intimacy! On which he will say, instead of me, Macchindranath will marry you. Then when he comes and marries you, you will get happiness. Since you have an affinity towards me, Macchindranath will be born from my illumination. And I will take re-birth as Meenanath, who will be your son from Macchindra. Then you will come in situ."

Everything had happened as per the curse of the Uparichar Vasu. She had come to the Kingdom of Women forgetting who she was. When the Queen there died, the elephant had crowned her as the Queen by putting a garland around her neck. Then she got married to Macchindranath and gave birth to Meenanath. That means she was close to the getting free from the curse. Mainakini had even got the name Kilotala.)

The bevy of Kalinga and Gorakshanath came to a village named Shrungamurud. Gorakshanath said to Kalinga, "Give me the work of playing the Mridangam*!" Kalinga said, "If you take the form of a woman only then can you come with us. There is a dance performance in front of the Queen." Then Goraksha took the form of a woman with the help of his Mantra power. He started looking much beautiful than Kalinga! Everyone gathered to perform in front of the Queen. Macchindra was sitting on his throne. Next to him was Mainakini and Meenanath was sitting in The performance started and the instruments started playing.

That time Goraksha played the Mridangam in such a way that its sound obviously matched the dancer?s performance but also made people feel like someone saying, „Come along Macchindra, Goraksha is here!? Listening to that voice Macchindranath startled. Kalinga?s dance performance inflamed! Everyone was engrossed in the performance. It seemed like the Mridangam was repeatedly reminding Macchindra, "Macchindranath! Let?s Go! Goraksha has come to take you along!" Macchindra?s facial expressions changed! He appalled! The Queen asked him, "What is happening to you?" He said, "The Mridangam is rippling, Goraksha is here! What if Gorakshanath comes here in reality?" The Queen asked the female playing the Mridangam straight away, "Are you rippling in that way purposely?" She said, "I don? t know! May be the other instruments need to be tried!" The same words came out from other instruments as well. Everyone was surprised! The Queen realized that Goraksha is amongst the group. She told the female playing the Mridangam, "This is something bizarre! You swear on your Guru and tell me who you really The performance had stopped by now.

That beautiful female replied politely, "Oh Mother, I am not a woman, I am Goraksha! I am a disciple of Macchindranath and have come here to take him along!" Macchindra told him, "Come in front of me in your original form." Then Goraksha emerged as a male.

Macchindra hugged him instantly! What a divine meeting that was!
Then Goraksha told him all that had happened during his travel and his
practice of asceticism. He held Meenanath and Goraksha close to him
on both sides.Everyone got engrossed in appreciating them.

Fruition: The recitation of this chapter will help get rid of mental
illness and the reader will live a happy married life.

***Mridangam** - A percussion instrument from India of ancient
origin.

MACCHINDRA'S EXIT FROM THE KINGDOM OF WOMEN

As per Lord Hanuman's suggestion Mainakini pampered Goraksha like a mother does to her child. But he didn't get overwhelmed by her caressing. Whenever he got an opportunity he incited Macchindra to leave from there. "I will leave this town and come with you", Macchindra took vows every time. One night Macchindra told Mainakini, "Goraksha is saying that he will take me away from here."Next day Mainakini told Goraksha, "You and Meenanath should now take care of this Kingdom together. We give all our powers to you! We will take refuge under your rule. Even if we get food and clothing we would be okay! You rule the Kingdom! And also take care of Meenanath." Goraksha said, "What do I have to do with these things? I am taking Guruji on a pilgrimage!" Mainakini asked him to stay back for six months till Padwa*.

After that he can leave; to which he agreed. In those six months she tried making him fall for various covetous and fascinating things like women, wealth, exotic food, beverages and clothing. But none of that had any effect on him. A beautiful young girl with the game of draughts was sent to Goraksha, to play with him. She tried subduing him in all possible ways but even in that case he didn't lose.

Heremained abstained Six months later the festival of Padwa came and there was happiness in the air. But Mainakini was sad. Now Macchindra was going to leave with Goraksha for sure. His adoration had proved more powerful than her love.

She was extremely upset and sad with the thought of her husband's separation. The same day Goraksha kept in front of Macchindra, a Zholi, Shingy, etc the various attributes of the Nath community and said, "Guruji, take this costume! We should leave now!" Mainakini requested Goraksha with tears in her eyes, "At least have food and then leave." Both of them agreed to her request.

After thinking for a while she said, "You should also take Meenanath along. He will not be happy here without you." Even Meenanath agreed to go with them. Nath decide to take him along. When they were leaving the palace, Mainakini kept a gold brick in Macchindra's Zholi without Goraksha knowing about it. She thought, on their way in troubled situations it will prove useful. Goraksha left without the women in the village knowing. Mainakini followed them and kept pleading to Goraksha. She was trying to keep her husband and son in vision as much as possible.

Goraksha left hurriedly so that she could get control over her grief. He told Macchindra, "Guruji you should get away from this entanglement as soon as possible." He told Mainakini, "You wait here till the time Uparichar Vasu comes here. He will free you from here." The three of them crossed the border of the Kingdom. A thought came to Goraksha's mind, "A Guru who should free his disciple from the worldly pleasures, but he has himself got entangled in it! For the friendship of Lord Hanuman his ascetic life got the stain of the nuisance of worldly pleasures." There Mainakini had started wailing and weeping. She kept lamenting hugging Macchindra's clothes and Meenanath's toys.

At that time the Uparichar Vasu was travelling in a plane in the cosmos. He heard her wail and got the plane near to the earth. He said to Mainakini, "You are free from the curse now. I have come to take you back to the Sinhala Island!" Mainakini stood aghast! She had forgotten that she is Padmini, not Mainakini and had come there due to the curse!

Fruition: The recitation of this chapter will help rid off the sin of killing the cow in last birth and the reader will get place in the Tapolok*

*__Padwa__- Hindu festival; Tapolok - A spiritual planet.

WASHED MEENANATH BUT DISPELLED GORAKSHA'S ILLUSION

The Uparichar Vasu reminded Mainakini of her actual name and the Sinhala Island. He told her, "All this happened to you due to the curse. Now I am going to take you to the Sinhala Island. You should stay in situ. After twelve years Lord Indra will perform a Yajna which will be attended by the Navnath's and the Gods! That time Macchindranath and Meenanath will meet you.

Make your maid named Dairbhama the Queen." Saying this Uparichar Vasu made all arrangements and took her to Sinhala Island. After which he went in situ.On the other hand, Gorakshanath, Macchindranath and Meenanath left on a pilgrimage. They reached the same mango grove where Kaanif had given Goraksha the news of Macchindranath being in the Kingdom of Women. Goraksha bowed down in adoration of that land and took Macchindra to Helapattan where he introduced him to Mainavati. She welcomed them. She reported to them the scene of Jaalandharnath and Gopichand. They stayed there for three days and then left for Jagannathpuri. From there they moved to Saurashtra visiting various towns on their way.

There in a village Goraksha had gone to solicit alms. They were staying on the bank of a river out of the village. When Goraksha returned, Macchindra said, "I have left Meenanath on the other side of the river to defecate. You take him to the river. I am going to the village." As instructed Goraksha went near Meenanath and saw that his full body had become dirty. An innocent child! Goraksha took him to the river and washed him as if one washes clothes. He banged him on a stone and then dunked him in water. The child died! He threw the child's blood and flesh in the water for the fish to eat. He thought he had done a benevolent act! He peeled the skin and washed it nicely.

Now I have washed the child clean he thought and kept it on the roof to dry.

Macchindranath returned from the village and asked, "Goraksha, how are you sitting so relaxed? Where is Meenanath?" "I cleaned him and have kept him there on the roof to dry!" said Goraksha. Macchindranath couldn't control his grief and fury! He hugged the skin and started crying uncontrollably.

He also started abusing Goraksha. On which he replied, "Guruji, why are you lamenting so much? Why such affinity towards this perishable life! Why are you even getting angry on me? What happened to your state of asceticism? Okay then, take your son!" saying this he chanted a mantra on the ash and threw it on the skin. Meenanath vivified! He hugged his Goraksha said, "Guruji you could have vivified him with the help of the Sanjeevani Mantra. Then why did you kept crying needlessly.

You are an ascetic! Don't you know Meenanath is just a phantasm for namesake? Then On that Macchindra said, "You are just now crossing the boundaries of this illusionary world! If the body of Meenanath is an illusion, then isn't my crying also an illusion? And when his illusionary body got dirty why did you feel disgusted? Won't the dirt also be an illusion? Killing Meenanath, being happy to have fed the fish, feeling of being benevolent, all this is also a part of the illusionary world.

Whatever you felt was right and when I cried for Meenanath, then he's just an illusion?" Goraksha stood aghast! He realized what his mistake was! Macchindra had got married just to release Lord Hanuman from the vow. All that had happened had not affected Macchindra's ascetic life! Realizing that Goraksha felt ashamed! He thought to himself, "It's my delusion to have thought that I pulled out my Guru from the worldly pleasures!" He touched Macchindra's feet and said, "Guruji it's my fault!" Macchindra replied, "I tested you! Now don't feel bad about it!"

Fruition: The recitation of this chapter will help give birth to a knowledgeable son and he will be accepted even by the scholars.

THE GOLD BRICK AND MACCHINDRA'S STORY

Goraksha, Macchindra and Meenanath went towards South. On the way was a dense forest. Macchindra said, "It's scary to even enter this jungle." Goraksha pacified him but thought to himself, "Why is my Guru so scared? He must be carrying some valuable! Otherwise why would a Yogi like him get scared?" Then Macchindra handed over Meenanath and his Zholi to Goraksha and left saying, "I am taking a different route. See you near the lake!" Goraksha peeped into the Zholi and found a gold brick in it and at once realized that this was the reason for Macchindra's fear. He threw that brick in the grass and kept a stone of the same weight in the Zholi. Later he reached near the lake along with Meenanath. At the same time even Macchindra reached there, taking a different route. He took back the Zholi and checked. He put his hand inside and found a stone. Goraksha asked, "That was the reason for your fear, wasn't it?" Macchindra replied, "You did a catastrophe!" He showered Goraksha with a spate of angry words.

At that time Goraksha chanted a mantra and threw ash on the nearby mountain. The entire mountain turned into gold! Macchindra said to Goraksha, "You are the real philosopher's stone!" Goraksha asked, "Why had you kept the brick with you?" Macchindra replied, "I had planned to give a feast to many sages!" Goraksha said, "That's all, right! I will do the arrangements for the same!" and called the demigod, Chitrasen with the help of a mantra. He told him, "Send all demigods to invite all Yogis' and God's along with Macchindranath for a divine feast." Accordingly Chitrasen called all God's, Rishi's, Yogis, Charon*, Demigods, the God of Karma, Lokpaal*, Dikpaal*, the Trinity and all other Gods. Riddhisiddhi prepared delicious food and Macchindra gave a very big feast.

That time Goraksha remembered Gahini. Taking Macchindra's permission he decided to call him. Gangabai and Madhu, the Brahmin was nurturing Gahini in their house. Macchindra sent a letter along with the Demigod Surochan to call the Brahmin along with Gahini.

The illuminated Brahmin Madhu, introduced Gahini to Goraksha and Macchindra and also told him; "Goraksha was the one who handed you over to me". Gahini bowed to everyone. He also got the opportunity of worshipping Lord Shankar. He said while patting down Gahini's back, "Karbhajan Rishi has incarnated in this body! Later I am going to incarnate as his disciple. So give me initiation now itself!"Goraksha gave the Secret Mantra to Gahini in the presence of Lord Shankar and many other Gods.

It was decided that in the presence of Lord Shankar, Gahini will learn Yoga for a year. The illuminated Brahmin Madhu went back leaving Gahini behind. After a year it was decided to send Gahini back to him. Then Goraksha told Lord Kuber, "Take to heaven this Mountain which has been turned into gold. Give clothes and jewelry enough to bid adieu to the people present here." Lord Kuber said, Let this mountain be here. I will provide all the clothes and jewelry. This mountain will remain invisible." Then all the guests were honored with the clothes and jewelry given by Lord Kuber and they took Macchindra's leave. The Uparichar Vasu took Meenanath to Sinhala Island. He met Padmini aka Mainakini and gave Meenanath to her. He also told her, "Soon Macchindranath will also meet you!" Along with Lord Shankar, Gahini and Goraksha stayed on the Garbhadri Mountain for a year.

After completing the Yoga lessons, Gahini was sent back to the illuminated Brahmin. The Garbhadri Mountain became invisible! Lord Shankar stayed there in the form of Giridevata*. He got the name Mhatardev, The Lord Vriddheshwar! After many years Macchindra and the other Nath's took Samadhi near Garbhadri.

Fruition: The recitation of this chapter will help preserve the gold in the house.

****Charon**- The ferryman of Hades who carries souls of the newly deceased;

Lokpaal- Guardian deities of the people, **Dikpaal**- Guardian deities of the directions; **Giridevata**– The Mountain God.

THE STORY OF BHARTARI'S BIRTH

The divine vision of Urvashi aroused Lord Sun's power of creation. A part of it fell in the pot kept in Lomash Rishi's ashram* and from that was born Agatya. The other part fell in a bhartari* kept in the porch of Kaulik Rishi's ashram. He preserved that part of Lord Sun's illumination in the same bhartari till the onset of Kali Yuga. And when it did, he shifted that bhartari in a cave on the Mandar Mountain. At that place the honeybees constructed a hive. Drumil Rishi entered that bhartari in the form of life. And that baby came out of the cave in sometime. He fell on the grazing field and started crying. A doe came there grazing and gave birth to two fawns. It felt that this child is also her own. The doe gave its udder in his mouth and taught him to drink milk.

It nurtured that child and that is how he learnt the language of animals. Even he started walking behind exactly like the doe on fourlegs.

Later a couple, Jaisingh and Renuka when passing by in the jungle saw this human child. They were marveled looking at this child's illumination and his walk like a deer. "He is for sure a human child! We should search for his mother and hand him over to her" thought Jaisingh. He went running to the child and picked him up. He started speaking to the child. But the child only kept bleating like a deer. Even the doe started making piteous bellows. Jaisingh was a Bhaat*. He decided to take the boy to his place where he was staying and they started walking hurriedly. The doe followed them for a long distance making piteous bellows but the poor being had to return from the jungle's border.

The boy started growing up at Jaisingh's house. They searched a lot for his mother but couldn't find her. How could they locate his mother who didn't exist in reality! The boy gradually learnt to stand on his feet and words of human language. They both started nurturing him, considering their own child.

Later one day they decided to visit Kashi to worship Lord Vishwanath. Accordingly they reached Kashi. They entered the Vishwanath temple along with that boy. Standing inside the shrine they joined hands and hailed, "Om Namah Shivay! Shambho! Jai Vishweshwar!" And a miracle happened! From the Shivalinga* came a loving and deep voice, "Welcome Bhartarinath*! DrumilNarayana, finally you descended in the Bhulok*!" Jaisingh and Renuka stood aghast! "This boy seems to be an incarnation! Lord Vishwanath himself called him Bhartari so we will give him the same name" they decided.

Jaisingh nurtured the boy as much as possible with utmost love and care. Days passed by and Bhartari turned sixteen years old. They had stayed in Kashi for all these years. On the way back to their village, a few thugs caught them. They robbed all their wealth and ran away after killing them. Bhartari had been somewhere away from them and so he was saved. He felt extreme grief at the death of his guardian parents. When he was crying a group of Vanjari* merchants were moving towards Avanti City with huge security. As they saw the boy crying, they came and consoled him. They thought, "This boy seems to be radiant and brilliant; he will be of use to us" and so took him along.

Soon he became everyone's beloved due to his characteristics. Those people did business in many villages and gathering a lot of mercantile moved towards Avanti city.

Fruition: The recitation of this chapter will destroy the sin of last birth's infanticide and own children will live a happy life.

*Ashram – Spiritual Hermitage; **Bhaat** – A Tribe; Bhartari - The vessel for receiving alms; **Bhartarinath** – Since he was born in a Bhartari he was named Bhartarinath; **Shivalinga** – A representation of the Hindu deity Shiva used for worship in temples; **Bhulok** – One of the seven heavens; **Vanjari** - Tribes of India who were in the past engaged in carrying grain and supplies for armies, before the time of cart-roads and railways.

SUROCHAN GANDHARVA

In the assemblage of Lord Indra, a Gandharva named Surochan misbehaved with Menaka, the nymph. And so Lord Indra cursed him, "You will be born in Mrityu Lok* as a donkey!" When he requested to take the curse back, Lord Indra said, "Even though you will be a donkey, you will remember your past, your Siddhis # will remain as it is, you will get married to the Princess Satyavati, daughter of the King of Mathura and you will have a son named Vikramaaditya. Only after that will you be free from the curse!" Surochan was born as a donkey.

A potter named Kamath found him and took him along. But at night he spoke to Kamath in a human voice, "My wife will be Princess Satyavati the daughter of this city's king, King Satyavarma! You shall get it done!"

Kamath felt amazement and fear at the same time. He got scared thinking of the big punishment he will get if the King comes to know of this. He loaded his pots on this donkey's back and left with his wife for another city. But on his way the guards on the city border stopped him for enquiry.

And since he didn't tell the reason, they took him to the King. It was not appropriate for his people to leave a happy city and so the King commanded, "Tell me the truth!" Kamath was a wise man! He said to the King, "I will tell you the reason secretly in private. But please do not get angry on me. I am not at fault! Please give me an assurance of my safety." The King took him to a secluded place and Kamath told him, "Your Majesty, my donkey talks at night in a human voice.

It keeps telling me to get the Princess married to it. If you come to know about this, you will punish me and so I was leaving this city. Please give your commandment without getting angry on me."

The King was a diplomat and a deep thinker. He made a conjecture that this is an accursed donkey and said, "You wait for tonight! If it says the same things again then tell him, if it turns our Mathura into a copper city only then is its marriage with the Princess possible." Kamath went home and the donkey said the same again that night. He gave the King's message. The donkey said, "At least he should have asked for a gold city! Tomorrow morning the entire city will be turned into a copper city. Tell the King to start with his daughter's marriage preparations."

Infact the next morning the entire city had turned into copper. Wood, mud, utensils, and every object had turned into copper. But thoughtfully it had kept the money and gold as it is! The donkey had appealed to Vishwakarma at night to do that work. All the people in the city were roaming around with surprise. Even the King marveled and thought this cannot be done without the help of a God.

He called Kamath! He told his daughter everything secretly, "Be courageous and wise! Your husband is an accursed God! He is now in the form of a donkey but soon he will take his original form." and convinced her for marriage. He told Kamath, "You take my daughter and leave this city. Otherwise it will be a reason for people's mockery."

Satyavati got ready to leave with Kamath and started crying a lot. So the King took her to the potter's house himself. When he saw the donkey, it said in a human voice, "King, I am a Gandharva* named Surochan. Due to Lord Indra's curse I have been born as a donkey. I have already got the boon and at the right time I will again turn into a Gandharva. You are getting your daughter Satyavati married to me which will help me free from the curse."

Listening to all that was said in a human voice cleared the King's doubt. He handed over Princess Satyavati to Kamath and his wife. That couple left Mathura the same night and left for Avanti city. The people didn't understand anything. Since the Princess herself was with them, they could easily cross the city's border.

Fruition: The recitation of this chapter will help get a human life in next birth, will help get a beautiful wife and one will never get affected by any curse.

*Mrityu Lok– Earth; Gandharva – Demigod.(Gandharvas can fly through the air, and are known for their skill as musicians.)

Siddhis - Siddhis are spiritual, magical, supranormal, paranormal, or supernatural powers acquired through a sadhana (spiritual practices), such as meditationand yoga . People who have attained this state are formally known assiddhas.

VIKRAM AND BHARTARI

Kamath started staying in a small house with his wife, his donkey and Satyavati in the city of Avanti. Once Satyavati said, "Father-in-law, can I ask you something? Why doesn't my husband pay attention to me? Why doesn't he speak to me in a human voice?" Kamath told her wish to the donkey, on which the donkey said, "When she will become matured enough for our union I will take the form of Gandharva and fulfill her wish." Kamath found it surprising but still he asked his wife to enquire about it. Sometime later she did and told Satyavati's condition to Kamath, who conveyed it to the donkey.

That night Surochan Gandharva showed his real form to Kamath, his wife and Satyavati. The entire room was illuminated. Everyone was aghast and very happy to see Gandharva's beauty. He embraced Satyavati. And in the same form, Surochan and Satyavati got married. He said, "Satyavati will beget a son from me. His name will be Vikramaaditya! Once our son is born I will go back to heaven!"

And as Surochan had said, after his son's birth a plane came from heaven to take him away. Satyavati started crying since her husband was leaving. He consoled her saying, "Even though I am going to the Heaven do not feel that our relation has ended. Whenever you remember me I will come to meet you from heaven and left.

In this way Surochan Gandharva had to come to earth due to the curse .and had to take birth as a donkey. But only because of that an emperor like Vikramaaditya was born!

With the love and affection of Satyavati and Kamath's wife, Vikramaaditya started growing up! He was basically a brilliant child. And so at a very young age he learnt many Vidya's. As soon as he grew up, due to the minister's acquaintances, he started getting work of collecting Octroi.

He helped the servants at the Octroi station. He was everyone's favorite due to his very good nature and characteristics.

One day, the group of merchants who had taken along Bhartari came near the border of that Kingdom. Bhartari had performed a mind blowing task on the way. The merchants were discussing about his act amongst each other. Bhartari had come to know from the foxes howl that a gang of robbers were going to attack their group and he alerted them. Due to which they had escaped the theft. Secondly, Chitrama Gandharva had got the birth of a Demon. Bhartari had prophesied whoever kills that Demon and puts a Tilaka* of his blood on the forehead and the main door of the town will become a King.

Vikram heard all this. He was a chivalrous youth! He went to the jungle the same night and killed the Demon. When the Demon died, Chitrama Gandharva came out of his body and gave Vikram the knowledge of all the gems inside the Demon's body. Then Chitrama left for Heaven. Accordingly, Vikram got the Amethyst, Chintamani, Diamond and Kamad gemstones. He put a Tilaka of the demon's blood on his forehead and also the main door of the town.

Vikram enquired from the merchant about Bhartari. He told Vikram, "Bhartari was alone in the jungle and so we took him along. He comprehends the language of animals. He is an extraordinary man!" They also gave a few other details.

Then Vikram and Bhartari met. They started liking each other instantly . He wanted Bhartari to be with him and to take him away from the merchants he did an idea. He sent a message with one of the Octroi collection servant for the merchants, "Bhartari's brother is calling him in the town. Send him! And since there is a relationship, we are remising the Octroi levied on your goods." Bhartari came as per the message. "Let him stay with me for some time. I will pay the Octroi" saying this Vikram called Bhartari to stay at his house. He gave one of the gem stone at the collection station as Octroi.

Satyavati told Vikram, "He is Bhartari! I have presumed him my brother. He is an orphan. I am going to ask him to stay with us!" And in this way Bhartari started staying with Vikram and his family.

Fruition: The recitation of this chapter will help get rid of the sin of killing cows and own children will not behave like enemies.

***Tilaka**- In Hinduism, the tilaka is a mark worn on the forehead.

THE MARRIAGES OF VIKRAM AND BHARTARI

A King named Shubhvikram was ruling the city of Avanti at that time. The Princess Sumedha had reached an age of getting married. The King spoke about it to his Chief Minister. "As per our traditional practice of searching for a son-in-law, giving a garland in the elephant's trunk we will make it roam around the city.

The person, around whose neck the elephant puts the garland, will become Sumedha's husband." The Chief Minister made arrangements accordingly. The elephant came roaming near the Octroi post and threw the garland around Vikram's neck. Vikramaditya was confused . Bhartari asked him to remain calm. The King , Chief Minister , Ministers and the other servants gathered around Vikram. Even the King came there and Vikram bowed in front of him. The King asked him his name and ancestral background. He was taken to the Kings assemblage with great honor. Bhartari told all this to Kamath and later even he was called with honor in the assemblage.

He gave the information, "Vikram is the son of Satyavati and Surochan Gandharva and Satyavati is the daughter of Mathura's King Satyavarma." The King Shubhvikram went to Mathura along with his Chief Minister. He met the King and confirmed the information. Then he got his daughter Sumedha and Vikram married lavishly. The King of Mathura also attended the wedding along with his huge family. The King Shubhvikram organized the coronation ceremony for Vikram. And later the new king, King Vikram pronounced Bhartari the Prince. Mathura's King also gave Vikram the right to rule his Kingdom. A few days later the Chief Minister thought that he should get his daughter Pingala married to Bhartari, who was the Prince and King Vikram's friend. Everyone liked his thought. But they didn't know of Bhatari's background. He was anenlightened soul , down to earth and learned , but it was difficult to know his ancestral background.

On asking Bhartari clearly, he told how Jaisingh and Renuka had nurtured him and how they were killed in the jungle. But he was actually born from Mitravaruna* inside a bhartari in a divine manner. The Chief Ministerraised a doubt, "How can we just believe blankly what you say?" So Bhartari went in the porch and looking at the sky urged Lord Sun, "Hey Mitravaruna, ifI am your inheritance then give your divine manifestation to the King's Chief Minister and tell him the truth!"

Hearing his son's call, Lord Sun manifested in a mild manner in the sky.The Chief Minister got extremely happy and felt blessed! Lord Sun said, "It's true that Bhartari is my son!" The Chief Minister told Lord Sun, "I am going to get my daughter married to Bhartari! If you come down for the wedding ceremony there will be no doubt in the minds of the people." Lord Sun replied, "No one will be able to bear my luminance.

I will send Surochan Gandharva for the wedding and I shall shower flowers from the sky. Then the people will be left with no doubt." And He went back upwards in situ.

Chief Minister was satisfied and he got Bhartari married to his daughter lavishly. Surochan Gandharva was present at the wedding, so everyone was assured about the background of Bhartari. And also there was a shower of aromatic divine flowers, so the atmosphere got filled with energy and excitement. Bhartari loved Pingala like crazy. They could not stay away from each other.

Lord Sun kept thinking of this, "Bhartari's birth was for a divine work. How will it be possible if he gets trapped in worldly pleasures?" While comparing Agastya's penance and Bhartari'sdetachment, he thought how he can take Bhartari on the path of renunciation . When he opened up about this to Lord Datta, he said, "I will make arrangement for Bhartari to enter the Nath community at the

righttime and will make him perform his duty of social upliftment."
Later, LordDatta manifested in front of Bhartari in a jungle and gave
him the idea of hisfuture work. Bhartari agreed to it and promised,
"Let me enjoy my married lifefor twelve years and then I will take
initiation." **Fruition:**The recitation of this chapter will help find a lost
thing and get back the lost rights.

*Mitravaruna** – Vedic name for Lord Sun.

BHARTARI AND PINGALA

Bhartari had given a promise to Lord Datta that he would take the path of renunciation after 12 years. He went home and all started seeing things in a

different light. His Avanti city, his prosperity, everything. It kept coming to his mind that one day he would be leaving all this behind.One day Pingala was taking rest on his lap. She said to him, "It will be great if I take my last breath while resting on your lap" He replied, "It?s difficult to tell what is in God? s mind? May be I will leave this world before you do!" She said, "Please don?t say that! I won?t be able to live even for a second after your death."

Bhartari took it as a joke and changed the topic. But when he went hunting, he decided to test Pingala? s love. He called his most faithful servant and gave him clothes drenched in deer?s blood. He told him, "You go to the palace in the city and tell them a tiger attacked and ate me up. I?ll give you my torn clothes and broken ornaments so everyone will believe it". He tutored his servant and sent him to the city after taking an oath from him to maintain secrecy.

Bhartari promised him of a big reward and hid behind some bushes without being noticed by other cavalrymen and hunters.

The servant narrated the made up story to the Queen as was ordered to him. Wiping tears, he even showed her Bhartari?s clothes. He went around telling everybody the same story.Pingala heard the news and saw those clothes.

Chaos spread everywhere in the palace. Pingala couldn?t bear the loss of her husband. She cried out loud and fell down on the floor lamenting. She decided to perform Sati and ordered the people to prepare the funeral pyre. She self-immolated along with Bhartari?s clothes. Her words, "Nath, I won?t be able to live after your death" had come true. Bhartari had no idea how disastrous his plan of testing her had proved to be.Bhartari returned at sunset along with his army.

Flambeaus were lit! Everyone reached the main door and the guards stunned! As soon as Bhartari entered the city, the people in a shocked state started telling him the horrendous story of Pingala?s death. He jolted! And realized what he had done! He went running to the crematorium where Pingala had done self-immolation and started crying out uncontrollably taking the ash from the pyre in People followed him and got him home.

The King Vikram, the Ministers and everyone else were mourning but still were trying to console him in all possible ways. He told everyone what had actually happened! He started repeating how he was responsible for Pingala?s death. Like a madman he started spending time at the crematorium. He gave up food and water and sat there chanting, „Pingala! Pingala!? Day by day his body became very weak.Looking at his condition even the others lamented. Twelve years passed by like this. Lord Sun and Lord Datta were watching all this. Lord Sun said, "Look at the condition of my son! Lord Datta, I hope you are watching?" He replied, "Gorakshanath is on a pilgrimage moving towards Avanti city. Just wait and watch! He will be the one to initiate him towards Moksha. Bhartari will become Chiranjiv!"

Fruition: The recitation of this Chapter will help get a virtuous girl for marriage and she will be of service lifelong.

Lord Shiva

Shivlinga

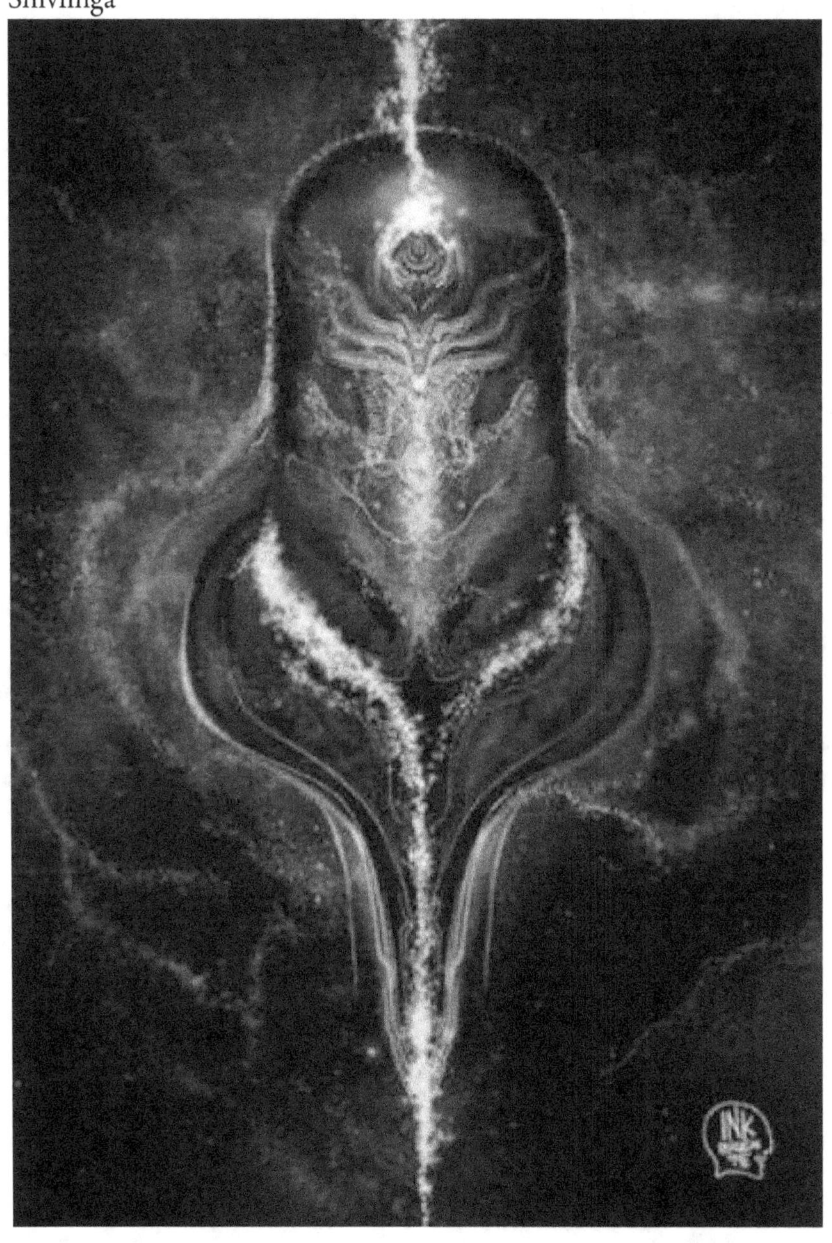

Lord Vishnu Story

The coming of the Navnath - or nine prophets - is mentioned in the Mahabharata. Krishna called a meeting of all demi-gods, angels and saints to give his message of how he would continue his message of spreading good after his mission is over on earth. Krishna said he would send his own light in the form of nine saints or prophets, who will go to different parts of earth and throughout the universe where life exists. Lord Krishna also mentions that these prophets or saints will spread the message of Love, overcoming obstacles in order to unite with Mahavishnu or Shiva or Shakti. Krishna said that they would help only those who have good souls and believers

The *Navnath Sampraday* or 'Navnath Parampara', is a Hindu sampradaya or parampara based upon the lineage of the Navnaths. The Navnath sampradaya spreads the message of Krishna that God exists everywhere and not just in a particular form or lack thereof. The Avatar of Dattatreya (Unified form of the trinity) came on the mission on earth to dispel confusion of earthlings who thought the three are different.

The teachings of the Nath Sampradaya have, over the centuries, become labyrinthine in complexity and have assumed different forms in different parts of India. Its teaching emphasises that the Supreme Reality can be realised only within the heart.In the day-to-day instructions to their devotees the Nath Gurus seldom refer to the metaphysics discovered by the scholars in their teachings.

GORAKSHA AND BHARTAR

After completing Macchindranath?s wish of feasting the Sages, Gorakshanath left to make a pilgrimage. As he reached the Girnar Mountain, Lord Datta welcomed him. He said, "My disciple named Bhartari is lamenting in Avanti city for the past twelve years due to his wife, Pingala?s death. He was going to be ready to take Sannyasa after twelve years. He is the Drumil Narayana! You use some tactic to stop him from lamenting

And introduce him to the Nath community!" As ordered Gorakshanath chanted the Yanaastra* and reached Avanti city at the speed of air. When he saw Bhartari at the crematorium, he got startled on seeing his skeleton body. „How weak a person becomes when in grief!? he thought. Goraksha started thinking how to get him out of that zero state. And he got an idea! He went to the city and bought an earthen pot

He drew a human face on it in a way that it looked like a doll. He took the doll and went to Bhartari. He dropped the pot purposely and pretended as if he stumbled. As soon as the earthen pot broke he started wailing, "My Doll! My Doll! My love, My Doll! Why did you leave me and go!" Saying this he collected the broken pieces and started rolling on the ground

Bhartari started wondering looking at his childish madness. He started consoling him, "It?s just an earthen pot! How costly would it be! Buy a new one! Why are you crying for something that you?ll get in a penny?" But Gorakshanath continued weeping in grief and said, "You are crying for your only wife! I love my doll similarly the way you love your wife!" Bhartari said, "I will get you a new earthen pot! Why do you have to cry? How can you compare a lively woman to a lifeless earthen pot? You?ll get thousand pots like this one!" Goraksha replied, "Then listen to this! You lost your Pingala; I will get your Pingala here to meet you but will also get thousand other Pingalas. You bet?" Bhartari said, "I will give you my Kingdom!

On that Gorakshanath pretended to wipe tears and taking the ash in hand he chanted the Sanjeevani Mantra and made Pingala alive. He also chanted the Kaamini* Mantra and appealed for duplicate thousand Pingala. At once Pingala came from Heaven and consoled Bhartari, "Nath I am living a happy life in Heaven. Why are you in so much sorrow? Although I have come down with the power of Gorakshanath?s Yoga, I will have to return! You please do not be in sorrow!" Thousands of Pingala that had surrounded her vanished

Bhartari touched Goraksha?s feet. Goraksha said, "Now tell me! What do you want? Pingala, the Kingdom or would you like to initiate on the path of Moksha?" Bhartari now agreed that the Power of Yoga is greater than the materialistic things like a wife or the Kingdom. He said with determination, "Please make me your disciple. I am finding all this very mundane.

Gorakshanath confirmed if his decision was final and gave him Yoga Diksha along with Kaanmantra*. The weak Bhartari stood up wearing the attire of the Nath community

Goraksha asked him to first go and solicit alms from the other women. Bhartari obeyed his orders! Leaving behind all the love and worldly pleasures he came back to Goraksha. He chanted the Shakti Mantra* and put ash on Bhartari?s body and forehead. At once Bhartari felt alive! Later they both went to the Girnar Mountain to meet Lord Datta, where Lord Datta took Bhartari close to him. Now was the time for the commencement of the work for which Drumil Narayana had incarnated. Gorakshanath had done the work of the Nath community with wisdom and tactics

Fruition

The recitation of this chapter will cure Tuberculosis and various other fevers

***Yanaastra**

The mantra to create a vehicle; Kaanmantra – The secret; Kaamini Mantra – The mantra of wish fulfillment; Shakti Mantra – The mantra of power

SHASHANGAR AND KRISHNAGA

Lord Datta gave Bhartari all the Siddhi and helped him attain the title „Chiranjiv?. He sent Gorakshanath to call Macchindranath from the Garbhadri Mountain. Goraksha went there and they both started their return journey to Girnar. On their way was Kaundinyapur, where they saw a young man laid down groaning at the city square. He was the Prince Krishnagar. The King Shashangar cut his hands and legs in anger and had thrown him there. When both the Naths enquired, they got to know of a strange story

The King Shashangar was barren for many years. He decided to make the Ministers responsible to handle the Kingdom affairs and stay at Rameshwar in South. He left with his wife Mandakini. On the way he stayed in a village at the confluence of the rivers Krishna and Tungabhadra. That night in his dreams he got the divine vision of the Lord Panchamukhi Shankar and he said, "King, at the confluence of both rivers you will get the Shiv Linga* and an idol of Aparna*. Bring it home and worship it, which will help you attain a son." As seen in the dream, the next day the King found a Shiv Linga and an idol of Parvati

The people were shocked. The King did the Prana Pratishtha* of that idol and built a temple for it. He regularly worshipped the idol in that temple. People started calling that deity, Sangameshwar. There the King found a baby boy in a miraculous way

At the same place resided a Brahmin named Mitracharya and his wife Sharayu. Even they were a barren couple. Lord Shankar was sitting on Kailash Mountain when he called the fairy Surochana for entertainment of his guards. While dancing she felt attraction towards Lord Shankar. He got furious and ordered her to take birth as a baby girl to that Brahmin

The fairy felt sad. She asked for the mitigation of the curse. Lord Shankar said, "Even there you will worship me. I will give you divine vision and will touch you. That is when you will turn into a fairy again.

Mitracharya gave birth to a baby girl and named her Kadamba. She was as beautiful as a fairy. Since childhood she had extreme adoration for Lord Shankar. She visited the temple regularly with her parents. One day she went to the temple alone and on her way back Lord Shankar gave her Divine vision. She got scared seeing him and started running. Lord Shankar caught her at the bank of river Krishna. To free her from the curse, when Lord Shankar held her hand, her body disappeared and she went to Heaven in her original form. An illumination fell from the body of Lord Shankar into the flowing Krishna River.

At the same time, King Shashangar was standing in the river. To perform Aaragya* to the Lord Sun he took some water in his cupped hands. Lord Shankar? s illumination which had come flowing with water came into his hands and as soon as it touched the King?s skin a beautiful baby was formed out of it

The King was surprised! "I have got this child due to Lord Shankar?s blessings exactly the way I had seen in my dream" saying this he kept praising Lord Shankar every now and then. He gave the child to Mandakini and they both came back to their original city happily. They had got that child in the Krishna River and so they named him Krishnagar

Mandakini passed away after some years. Krishnagar was only seventeen years old then. The King saw a lot of girls for his son to get married but didn?t like any. Even the King was a widower so he decided to get married himself. He got married to the Princess Bhujawati, daughter of King Bhujadwaj from Chitrakut. Princess Bhujawati was thirteenfourteen years old

Because of this Queen Bhujawati, Krishnagar had got into a big trouble. The Queen had seen Krishnagar just once at the time of her marriage. One day when the King had gone hunting, Queen Bhujawati saw Krishnagar while he was flying a kite. His handsomeness aroused her. She didn?t know that he was her husband?s son. She felt so lustful that she called him to her palace through her most faithful maid. When he came, she told him her desire in private. But he had become cautious on seeing her gaze. He said, "You are my mother! How can you ask something so weird? This is a sin!" He did not wait there even for a second

As he left, Queen Bhujawati got scared and she called her maid. On telling her the entire scene, she said, "Your Highness, don?t you be sacred! I?ll tell you a trick!

Fruition

The recitation of this chapter will blind the thieves

Shiv Ling

- A representation of the Hindu deity Shiva used for worship in temples;

Prana Pratishth

- The actual invocation ceremony meaning life-breath by which the sacred image of God is brought to life through chanting Mantras, hymns and offering prayers;

Aaragy

– Offering water to the sun at dawn;

Aparn

– Anothername of Goddess Parvati

MERCY ON KRISHNAGA

Bhujawati?s maid told her, "Do as I tell you, now you pretend to be very upset and sleep in your palace. Do not get up even if the King comes. He will enquire about you and will try to console you. Then you tell him, when he had been hunting his son tried to rape you. Also create and tell him a false story of how he tried to force you into it

Then he will believe in you and will punish him." Bhujawati did as told by the maid! When the King came she parroted the entire fuss as directed by her maid. As soon as the King got to know of his young son?s wrongful act he ordered, "Cut off both his hands and legs! Also tie him on a wooden bedstead and throw him at the city square." Though the servants found this punishment ruthless they had no option but to do it. This way the young boy was squirming at the city square. The sun was shining bright and he was experiencing excruciating pain

The people around were mocking. Some were saying the King is at fault, a few said the Queen is at fault and few said its Krishnagar?s fault

Gorakshanath and Macchindranath had recognized with their clairvoyance that it was Bhujawati?s complot. They felt pity for Krishnagar since he had been a victim to injustice. They decided to go to the King and ask for his custody. They met the King accordingly and gave a prelude by taking a promise that he will not deny their small proposal. They said, "Can we take your crippled son Krishnagar along with us. He will be useful to us!

The King started laughing and said, "Take him along if you wish to. It?s up to you! You will have to serve him! Of what use can he be to you?" Macchindranath said, "We will see what to do! You just donate him! We have decided of what use he will be to us!" Nath was extremely furious at the King. They wanted Krishnagar himself to punish the King and Queen

In the middle of the city square the King ordered his servants, "Hand Krishnagar over to these sages!" Both the Nath?s picked him up and with utmost care took him out of the city. They applied natural medicines on his wounds. They washed him clean, and fed him fruits with love. Krishnagar saw their love and started crying

In a span of just two three days due to Nath?s caring, loving and innocent nature Krishnagar felt at ease. He felt like he is in safe hands now. Both the Naths took him to Badrikaashram and kept him in a deep cave nearby. That cave had an opening at the top. They kept him inside the cave and said, "We are going to close the cave entrance with a huge rock. You keep an eye on it! So that it will not fall. If you move your eyes from it, it will fall on your head and you will die

You will get fruits to eat!" Goraksha gave him a Mantra to chant and keeping the rock on the cave entrance they left. Goraksha asked Goddess Chamunda to keep enough fruits in front of Krishnagar every day. Later they both went to Girnar Mountain and met Lord Datta

Macchindranath and Gorakshanath named Krishnagar, „Chaurangi?. He was in a very complicated condition. The wounds on his hands and feet hadhealed but he couldn?t move his eyes from the rock. Since he had no hands, if he had to eat the fruits kept in front of him with his mouth he would have to bend down and hence move his eyes from the rock. That meant he stayed starving! He was chanting the Mantra continuously and so his senses became focused

As days passed he weakened. His body got covered with anthill. Chanting of the Mantra kept inspiring him

Fruition

The recitation of this chapter will obstruct any ill-effects if any of Sabari Mantra from affecting oneself

THE KING TRIVIKRAM WITH MACCHINDRA'S SOUL

Macchindra and Goraksha stayed on Girnar Mountain with Lord Datta for some days and with his permission moved on to make a pilgrimage. When they reached Kaashi, the King Trivikram had just died and the King's people were in grief. Goraksha said, "It seems this King was a very nice man. If we vivify him, his people will be happy again." Macchindra said, "The King is in Heaven now

And it's not possible that he will return." They were sitting in a temple on the outskirts of the city. When discussing, the King's funeral procession passed by. When Goraksha again took out the topic, Macchindra said, "I'll play a trick! I will leave my body and enter the King's body. You take care of my body till then.

Goraksha was very happy! Macchindra entered the King's body and the corpse starting moving. The people were shocked. They cancelled the funeral and took the King with lot of respect to his palace.By then Goraksha took help of the priest's wife and secretly kept Macchindra's body in the basement at the backside of the temple

He told the priest's wife, "This body belongs to the great sage Macchindra. It will last for twelve years. But you should not tell this to anyone. Promise me!" She agreed to it. But she had come to know that Macchindra had entered the King's body. The basement was locked and Goraksha stayed in the temple

The people were thinking that the King had revived to life. All the King's life secrets were known to Macchindra so nobody felt suspicious. Macchindra who was in the King's body kept worshipping Lord Shiva exactly the way the King did. So the Queen Revati didn't find it suspicious. One day Macchindra went to the temple and took assurance from Goraksha if his body was safely kept

Three months later Goraksha went on a pilgrimage.Sometime later Revati got pregnant and delivered a baby boy when the time was due. They named him Dharmanath. One day the Queen came to the temple along with her son. After worshipping the idol she prayed to Lord Shankar. "Lord Mahadev, now my last wish is to die a Suvasini*.

The priest's wife was present there at that time. She knew the secret and so she laughed. The Queen asked the reason for her laugh. At the same time the King came and took away their son from the Queen. The priest's wife told the actual story secretly and the Queen went in a shock and fainted. There were still seven years left for Macchindra to leave the King's body. But what, after that? She will become a widow

The Queen decided to destroy Macchindra's body. She made the priests wife open the basement door and asked her servants to cut Macchindra's body into pieces and throw them in the jungle. The Queen got it done from the servants secretly in her own presence. She threatened the priest's wife and also made her swear. Now the Queen was sure that Macchindra will not be able to leave the King's body

Goddess Parvati was watching all this. She told Lord Shankar the entire scene. Lord Shankar asked Goddess Parvati to send the lady guards to collect and keep the pieces of Macchindra's body. The lady guards went along with Goddess Chamunda to collect the pieces and gave it to Veerbhadra on Goddess Parvati's orders. Macchindranath had earlier defeated these Matrukas and Veerbhadra too

That time Veerbhadra thought the great sage Gorakshanth might come to Kailasa looking for Macchindranath. He kept the pieces of his body in custody of lakhs of Lord Shiva's guards. He decided, even if Gorakshanath comes, he should not get those pieces

In Kashi, Macchindra continued to stay in the King's body and looked after the affairs of his Kingdom for seven years. Goraksha was on a pilgrimage. Whenever Macchindra came to the temple he would just roam around the entire temple. On seeing the closed door of the basement he would feel relaxed with the thought that his body was safe inside

Fruition

The recitation of this chapter will vanish the misfortune and will get a long lif

***Suvasini**

A term of courtesy or politeness for a woman whose husband is alive

ADABANGANATH AND CHAURANGINATH; RE-ARRIVAL OF GORAKSHANATH

While on a pilgrimage Gorakshanath was passing by the River Godavari. At one place he saw a farmer having breakfast in his field. Goraksha was hungry and thirsty so he asked for some bread. He felt satisfied on having the bread and drinking some water given by the farmer. And he said to him, "I am a sage! You have given me food and water

I will grant you a wish!" The farmer's name was Manik, he replied, "You asked for food and water from me! What can you give me? Instead ask from me if you need anything else." Gorakshanath caught him in words and said, "Please do the following, don't do whatever you would like to do! Just listen to this much!" Manik replied, "Okay!" Then Manik kept standing at the place he was. He kept neglecting all the thoughts that came to his mind

In this way Goraksha gave the farmer the Diksha* of impassiveness and went to Badrikaashram. He moved the rock kept on the cave entrance where Chaurangi was kept. Gorakshanath could hear the chanting of the Mantra from inside the anthill. With the power of his Yoga he alerted Chaurangi. He was about to die but had grown hands and legs due to the power of Yoga. Goraksha with his clairvoyance revived him

Later they met Lord Shankar and he taught Chaurangi all the Vidyas. And put power into his Mantras by taking blessings from all Gods. Chaurangi was now an accomplished man! Krishnagar had now become Chauranginath! Then Goraksha said, "Now we will go to Kaundinyapur." Both of them chanted the Prayanaastra and with the speed of air arrived near Kaundinyapur from the sky. To teach King Shashangar and Queen Bhujawati a lesson they used the Vaataastra* and kept all the servants who were in the palace and its garden, rotating and hanging in the air

When the King enquired about it they used the Vaataastra and Parvataastra* to force him capitulate

Then Krishnagar introduced himself to his father. The King became happy. He invited Gorakshanath and Chauranginath aka Krishnagar in the city. That time Krishnagar told the King about the complot, Queen Bhujawati had planted. The King got extremely furious and abandoned the Queen from the city. Only after that Gorakshanath and Chauranginath entered Kaundinyapur. From there they both left for Kashi. Gorakshanath wanted to see if Macchindranath's body was in the basement. But the priest wife told him the Queen's act and touched his feet for forgiveness

Gorakshanath opened the Gorakshanath told everything to Chaurangi and said, "I am going to take Yogasamadhi* and with a micro body search for my Guru in fourteen mansions. Till then keep my body safe in this basement. Prevent it from falling into the same situation like Macchindra's body." Then Goraksha in his micro form went in search of his Guru. After searching in seven Heavens and seven Hades he finally reached Kailasa! There he came to know that Macchindra's body is in custody of the Lord Shiva's gaurds and Veerbhadra

After that he returned to Kashi in his micro form. He entered his original body and came out of his Samadhi state. He got up and told Chaurangi, "Lets go! Now we need not stay here!"Both of them went to Kailasa. They tried their best to acquire the body of Macchindranath but Veerbhadra did not pay any heed to them. Ashtabhairavar*, the demons, Goddess Chamunda and Veerbhadra battled with them.

Fruition

The recitation of this chapter will keep one away from Tetanus, a medical condition and one who is already suffering will be cured

*** Diksh**

- An initiation by the Guru;

Vaataastr

–The weapon to bring about a gale capable of lifting armies off the groun;,

Parvataastr

– The weapon to cause a mountain to fall on the target from the skies

Yogasamadh

– A state where the person goes into Samadhi with the help of Yoga;

Ashtabhairava

– (Lord Bhairavar is the moving form of Lord Shiva) The eight Maha Bhairavar's controlling or guarding the eight directions of this

MACCHINDRA, DHARMANATH AND ADABANGANAT

Goraksha and Chaurangi gathered all the pieces of Macchindra?s body and reached Kashi. Macchindra was inside the King?s body. Goraksha met him and reminded that twelve years are about to get over. So he gave Dharmanath the responsibility of his Kingdom. He came to know of Queen Revati?s deed and she came to know of Goraksha?s valour. She immediately realized that now Macchindra will go away and made Dharmanath understand, "Biologically, Macchindra is your father!" In Lord Shiva temple Goraksha invoked Macchindra by chanting the Sanjeevani Mantra to come back into his own body. On the other hand Macchindra left the King?s body, entered his newly organized body and came to life. He stayed with Revati and Dharmanath for a month. "Goraksha will come back after twelve years to give you Diksha. Till then pay homage to your mother and enjoy your kingship", said Macchindra to Dharmanath and left on a pilgrimage with Goraksha and Chaurangi

Goraksha took Macchindra to Manik, the farmer on the bank of River Godavari and explained to him his situation. Macchindra went close to the farmer and said, "Manik let your ascetic practice complete." Manik replied, "Get lost from here!" Goraksha said, "Guruji, this man should be handled wisely!" Then he went close to Manik and said, "Wow! What a great ascetic he is! One should take Diksha from him!" On which Manik replied, "Diksha? You give me Diksha! Give me advice!" Recognizing his habit of back answering, Goraksha had got him to confess that. Immediately Goraksha gave him the Beejmantra of Diksha in his ears

Listening to that Divine Mantra, Manik got the revelation of Advaita. Chanting the Shakti Mantra Goraksha made him strong.

Manik was named „Adabanganath?. Nath made him proficient in Yoga Vidya. After that Nath went to Kashi and gave Diksha to Dharmanath. Dharmanath was a father now. He made his son the King and all the five Naths went on a pilgrimage. Dharmanath was given Diksha on Shuddha Dvitiya* and hence that Tithi* came to be called „Dharmanath Beej?. Gorakshanath promised, "On that day whoever gives a food feast to the people, Goddess Laxmi will inhabit in their house.

Chamas Narayana?s incarnation also happened in an extraordinary way. Lord Brahma?s illumination fell on earth in grass on the bank of River Reva. In that illumination Chamas Narayana Rishi entered in a life form and incarnated as a baby boy. A peasant was passing by and heard the baby crying. He thought to himself this is God?s gift and took him home. He gave the baby to his wife. The couple already had a son

They started nurturing both the boys together. The baby was found on the bank of River Reva and so they named him „Revan?. By the time he became twelve-thirteen years old he had learnt the work of a peasant

One day Revan was taking the bulls for grazing in the jungle. He got pushed by Lord Datta who was passing by the same road that time at the speed of air. Obviously Lord Datta?s touch made him realize that his original form is „Chamas Narayana?. He immediately hugged Lord Datta?s feet and requested him to give advice. Lord Datta felt, giving this youngster little Siddhi would be wise. So he kept his divine hand on the boy?s head and giving him milliequivalent Siddhi he disappeared.

Fruition

The recitation of this chapter will help get success in all walks of life

***Shuddha Dvitiy**

- One of the Lunar days, Tithi – A Lunar da

REVANNATH

After Lord Datta left, Revan thought of testing the Siddhi he had got and tried converting the heap of mud into gold with its help. On succeeding he asked, "Mother, will you fulfill my wishes?" She said, "I will do it remaining invisible" and she disappeared with the gold heap

Next day the peasant was asking Revan to go to the farm when he filled the house taking help of Siddhi Yoga with food grains, wealth, ornaments and clothes. Seeing Revan?s Siddhi, the peasant realized that this boy is a great sage and started taking care of his wishes. Then Revan started giving food to the villagers with the power of his Siddhi. The people started getting a good feast without any efforts. People started calling him „Revansiddhanath?

While travelling Macchindra came to that village and was staying at a hospice. People told him, "All villagers have their feast at Revansiddhi?s place

You will also get food over there." Macchindra intuitively recognized that Revan is a Chamas Narayan and Lord Datta has given a few Siddhis to him with the help of which he gives the feast. Then Macchindra created animals and birds with his Siddhis and made them play on his shoulder, fed them and freed them in the sky. Villagers narrated this to the Revan, so he came there

On seeing that, he asked his Siddhi about it. She Replied, "This is possible for those who have experience of Advaita." Revan asked, "Then give that experience to me too". She said, "This can be done only by Lord Dattatray." "I will surrender myself to him," saying this he went to the place where he had met Lord Datta. He started meditating with empty stomach with the wish to meet him again

Macchindra personally met the Siddhi of Revan to enquire about him. She said, "Lord Datta showed mercy on him and he appointed me to serve him." Macchindra understood that he shares brotherhood with

Revan as both have a same Guru. He went to the Girnar Mountain to convince his Guru and they both came to meet Revan

Then Lord Datta gave power to him and took him to the Girnar Mountain. He gave Revan all the Vidya and the Siddhi to make him an accomplished Sage and ordered him to go on pilgrimage

On the way to a pilgrimage, Revan reached Vite village which situated in the Maan country. At night he stayed there with a Brahmin family in their house. That couple had a tragic story. Their children didn?t survive! That day was the naming ceremony of their seventh child, but even he died in the function. It was a very tragic and sad situation! On hearing the couple?s grief Revan?s heart melted

He said to the Brahmin, "By mercy of Lord Datta I have acquired some Siddhi?s. I?ll go to Lord Yama to get back your son?s life. Please take care of his body for three days." Consoling them in this way he chanted the Amarmantra* and applied ash on the boys forehead. After which he went to Lord Yama in micro form with the power of Yoga. He asked to give back the life of the Brahmin?s boy from Vite Village. Lord Yama was aware of Revan?s abilities but was helpless due to the rules of the Universe and Karma. He told Revan, "I am doing my duty as per the rules. I do not have the right to give back the boy?s life. You should meet Lord Shankar. Only he can do this!" Considering whatever he said is right, Revan went to Kailasa

Fruition

The recitation of this chapter will help attain great Siddhi?s and forty-two generations will go through reformation

***Amarmantr**

-The mantra to remain immortal

REVANNATH AND NAAGNATH

Lord Shankar's guards battled fiercely with Revan. But finally everyone including the Lord fainted due to the effect of Vaataakarshan Mantra. When Gandharva called Lord Vishnu for help, Lord Vishnu asked Revan politely, "Revan, what is the reason behind the battle?" Revan said, "The seven sons of a Brahmin from Vite village died at a very young age. The Brahmin is extremely sad. I want to take away that Brahmin's sadness by making his sons alive again." Lord Vishnu said, "All those seven souls are in my contiguity

If you want to give them Sanjeevani then first prepare seven bodies." Revan agreed to it. He came back to Mrityulok and entered his own body. He narrated everything to the Brahmin. They wanted seven bodies. Revan prepared seven bodies from the body of the seventh son. With help of the Sanjeevani Mantra he put life into those bodies. All the seven souls came back from Heaven

Seeing the divine birth of their sons, the couple became very happy! Later Revan gave those boys Diksha of the Nath community. (Even today in Vite village Revannath has extreme respect.

How did Avirhotra Narayana incarnate

The illumination of Lord Brahma which came to earth was gulped by a female snake hiding in the trunk of a Banyan tree. The theist was aware of God's plan

He told the female snake that a sage will incarnate from inside you and safeguarded her. Later the snake laid an egg and it went away. From that egg was born a baby boy. A Brahmin named Koshdharma came there to collect the leaves of that Banyan tree to use as plates. He heard the cry of that baby boy. An oracle occurred, "Take this child home and nurture him. You will get bliss in it!" That Brahmin without any doubt in mind took the baby home. His wife Suradevi rejoiced! The couple named the baby Vatasiddha Naagnath and at the right time did his Munja. The Brahmin lived in Kashi city. This boy used to play in the

Vishveshwar temple along with other boys and would always pretend to serve food to them. Lord Datta took the form of a boy and asked the boys around, "I am a guest. May I come to have food?" Everybody said no but Naagnath pretended to serve food to him too

By seeing his hospitality Lord Datta immediately recognized that he is the Avirhotra Narayana. He said to Naagnath, "Henceforth whichever food you wish to eat will appear in front of you that very moment. And you will be able to serve food to these children in reality." Saying this Lord Datta in the form of a child went away from there

After that Naagnath would just wish for and the best of food would appear in front of the boys. All of them stopped eating at home. Everyone was surprised! Koshdharma Brahmin gathered all information from Naagnath and came to know that it's the grace of Lord Datta. He told Naagnath, "That boy was Lord Datta indeed!

Naagnath was desperate to meet Lord Datta. He left Kashi and also came to South. Someone told him, "Lord Datta comes to Kolhapur every afternoon to solicit alms, but secretly." So he thought that if he gives a feast to the whole village then no one will eat at their homes. And if Lord Datta didn't get any food in the village then he would also come there for the alms and could meet him

Naagnath met the temple priest and told him of his Siddhi. He expressed his wish to give a feast to the whole village. The priest was surprised. Naagnath was young but had an astonishing grace. The priest sent a message across the village for the villagers to come for a feast in the temple

Fruition

The recitation of this chapter will help cure snake bite and scorpion bite

NAAGNATH, LORD DATTA AND MACCHINDRA

Everyday in Kolhapur Naagnath would give a feast twice a day. He had the hopes that someday Lord Datta would come there to solicit alms from him and he would obtain his divine sight. One day Lord Datta arrived there and understood that Naagnath from Kashi is giving a feast here. He asked for arid alms and left. On enquiring, the people told Naagnath about a man who had asked for arid alms

Naagnath gave everyone some food grains. He said, "If anyone comes to ask for alms give him these food grains and tell him that these are given by Naagnath. And after telling him this, if he refuses to take alms, then inform me immediately

I have some very important work with that man." The next day a sage came to one of that person's house to solicit alms. That person gave him arid alms and said, "Due to the grace of the great sage Naagnath I have so many food grains in the house. And so I could give it to you!" On hearing this, the man moved back. The person in the house asked, "What happened? Why are you refusing the alms?" The man seeking alms replied, "I do not want food coming from that Naagnath!" People gathered around him. One of them went and informed Naagnath, "That man has come to solicit alms

He is not accepting the arid alms. He is saying I do not want food that has come from Naagnath." Naagnath went hurriedly and hugged the man's legs crying, "Guruji why did you leave me and go? You left me in a dense jungle! You met me in Kashi and then left me alone!

He was Lord Datta. He hugged Naagnath with love and took him along to a place where he gave him the Diksha of Knowledge. He made sure that supreme truth and knowledge took the place of his ignorance. In Kolhapur the feast preparations were done for the day. People came to know and felt sad that Naagnath will be leaving Kolhapur. But he was not going to wait! Lord Datta and Naagnath went to Kashi with the help of the Vyaanmantra* and worshipped Lord Vishwanath. After that they went to Badrikaashram which is the home to all ascetics and the most respected place of all sages. Lord Shankar recognized that he is Avirhotra and so gave him all the knowledge and made him an accomplished sage. He urged all the Gods to bless his Mantras and Weapons. After that as directed by Lord Datta, Naagnath went on a pilgrimage. And Lord Datta went to the Girnar Mountain

While on a pilgrimage, Naagnath reached the Vadvaal village. When meditating he would keep guards on the door of the monastery so that no one can disturb him. Macchindra came to the same village. The guards stopped him. Out of necessity he showed them the glimpse of his power. Naagnath had to come out and they met with unique love in their hearts. Then Macchindra asked him the reason behind having guards at the entrance. Naagnath replied, "I didn't want people's disturbance while meditating." Macchindra said, "Don't do that! We have incarnated to serve the people! Then how can you be unavailable for them? Let everyone have the freedom to meet you.

Accordingly Naagnath dismissed the guards and started solving people's problems. Once he vivified a dead man using the Sanjeevani Mantra as he felt pity for him. As this news spread people started getting corpses to him and rapidly people started coming back to life. Due to which Lord Yama's work was in complete disarray. He took his complaint to Lord Brahma who then came to meet Naagnath in micro form and dissuaded him from using the Sanjeevani Mantra frequently

Later Vatsiddha Naagnath took Samadhi.

Fruition

The recitation of this chapter will turn an indecisive and lose character person into a knowledgeable one.

Vyaanmantr

- A mantra for rapid movement

CHARPATINATH

Like all other Nath's even Pippalaayan Rishi incarnated in an extra-ordinary manner. The illumination of Lord Brahma had fallen on earth in which Rishi Pippalaayan entered and took the form of a baby. He laid there crying on grass. A Brahmin named Satyashrava came there to pick Darbha. He saw the baby and flowers started showering on him from the sky. The Brahmin found all that very spooky

Narada, the Vedic sage, came there in a sadhu's attire and told him, "Take this child home! There is nothing to be scared of. And name this child Charpati." He instructed! The Brahmin took him home, when he came to know that the child is an incarnated Rishi. The child grew up studying at the house of the Brahmin till he turned twelve years old. Narada saw that and went to Badrikaashram to ask Lord Datta, "It's been twelve years after Rishi Pippalaayan took birth as Charpati. When are you going to give him Brahmavidya and complete Siddhi?" Lord Datta replied, "No Brahmavidya without contrition. There is still time for all of that.

Narada was very concerned of Charpati! He took the form of a poor child and went to the Brahmins house. He pleaded, "Can I stay at your place for studies? I will do all the household work." The Brahmin agreed to take him home. Narada had changed his name to Kulamba and had taken the form of a boy of the same age as of Charpati. The Brahmin thought to himself, "The boy is good to do all the work and will also learn to solicit alms with Charpati." And soon all that he had thought came into reality. Narada aka Kulamba was continuously in search of an idea due to which Charpati will get angry on his family and will leave the house. And in a few days it happened

One day the Brahmin Satyashrava was called for at a gentleman's place for some religious ceremony. And since he didn't have time he sent Charpati. The man gave him lesser Dakshina* than usual. Charpati got into an argument with him but the man was not ready to listen.

Seeing them argue Kulamba came home and told Satyashrava. By then even he had got free from his work. "Come, let me see!" he said and took Kulamba along to that man's house. Charpati was still arguing. His father slapped him, gave him a piece of his mind and sent him home. "Please don't pay any attention to what my son said

We should be satisfied in whatever you give us with your own will," he said to the gentleman and asked for forgiveness. By that time Kulamba had left from there. Now there were clashes between the son and his father proving an opportunity for Narada

Instead of coming home, Charpati went to a temple on the outskirts of the village and sat there crying. Kulamba went to the Goddess temple and said things which would infuriate him, "We will not go home now! We are basically righteous and anyone can teach us the Vidya" saying this he managed to persuade Charpati and they both left the village and went on a pilgrimage

Sometime later they went to Kedarnath temple and sat there in meditation. While doing so Narada thought to himself, "This is the right time to show Charpati my original self." He was sitting as Kulamba when he invited Macchindranath with his Yoga power and said, "Charpati, open your eyes and see!" When Charpati opened his eyes he saw the huge and glorious Macchindranath

Also standing next to him was Narada having the Veena* in his hand. He recognized Narada as he had read of him in books. Narada said, "I had taken the form of Kulamba and he is Macchindranath" and Lord Datta gave Charpati his Divine vision and compassionately gave him Diksha. Lord Shankar also emerged in front of him. He asked Lord Datta, "Give him all the Vidyas and make him an accomplished sage." Lord Datta did accordingly and instructed Charpati to go on a pilgrimage

Fruition

The recitation of this chapter will help get rid of Malaria, Typhoid and similar diseases.

***Dakshin**

- Vedic concept of donation or payment for the services of a priest, spiritual guide or teacher;

Veen

- An Indian and Pakistani plucked stringed instrument used mainly in Indian classical music

CHARPATINATH'S SAGA

Charpati did all the pilgrimages on earth and went to Badrikaashram. He chanted the Vyanaastra Mantra with the wish to go to Heaven. First he went to Satyalok* and met Lord Brahma whose son he was. With love he asked Charpati to stay over with the sage Narada. One day when Narada had been to Lord Indra, he said mockingly, "Come, you stirrer! Narada, Come! What is going to be your next instigative plot?" Narada was fuming inside but smiled superficially and said, "Only when I instigate you, will I feel like being the real stirrer, Narada." Narada gave Charpati the Siddhi to move in the Trikhand*. They left to see Nandanvan where they ate the best fruits to their heart's content. They also got a lot of fresh flowers from there and bestowed upon Lord Brahma. He became very happy to see their love but he didn't know that those flowers were brought from Nandanvan

Everyday Narada and Charpati started going to Nandanvan to eat fruits. When the guards of the jungle noticed it they came running. Narada escaped and Charpati bothered the guards with the Vaataakarshan Mantra. A few other guards saw that and complained to Lord Indra, "A sage has forcefully entered Nandanvan and has almost killed many guards." Lord Indra sent an army of thousand guards on him. Seeing them raging Charpati chanted the Vaataakarshan mantra and made them unconscious

Hearing the entire scene, Lord Indra himself went to Kailasa on his Airavata*. He told everything that had happened to Lord Shankar and asked for his support. Lord Shankar told his messenger, "Ask Lord Vishnu to come prepared for a battle. This enemy seems extremely valiant." As soon as Lord Vishnu got the message he headed towards Nandanvan with his group of a crore soldiers

Charpati saw the two armies; Shiv's army and Vishnu's army coming from two sides of Nandanvan. So first he used the Mohiniastra* on the Sudarshan Chakra* and made it sluggish and immediately used the Vaataakarshan Mantra collectively to make Vishnu's army completely exhausted. Charpati took Lord Vishnu's necklace, his Gada* and his Chakra and gave it respectfully to Lord Brahma. He had also made Lord Shankar exhausted and motionless using the Vaataakarshan mantra

Lord Brahma was astonished to see Lord Vishnu's weapons and ornaments. He asked, "From where did you get all this?" Charpati replied with attitude, "When I had been to Nandanvan to get flowers for you, there came the guards of the jungle and of Gods. Also Lord Vishnu and Lord Shankar came along with their guards but I made all of them unconscious with help of the power of mantras. I have got these weapons of Lord Vishnu for you.

"What have you done? If Lord Vishnu and Lord Shankar do not do their work the whole world will pause. And if you spell a mantra on me the Universe will come to a standstill. Come to Nandanvan with me right now!" saying this the Creator took Charpati to Nandanvan and asked him to resume the consciousness of Lord Indra, Lord Shankar, Lord Vishnu and all the guards. When he did so using the Sanjeevani Mantra, Lord Brahma apologized to them for Charpati's wrong doing and made him apologize to them by touching their feet. Everyone was assured that he is the Sage Pippalaayan

At the same time Narada arrived and asked Lord Indra, "Oh, King of Gods! What happened to you? Hope you didn't come across any other Narada, a stirrer!" Lord Indra understood that this was the result of mocking Narada and so he apologized to him

Later for a year along with Narada, Charpatinath stayed near Lord Brahma. He then went to Hades and accepted the welcoming from King Bali. Thus, he saw all places in Heaven, on Earth and in Hades

Fruition

The recitation of this chapter will get victory in a battle.

***Satyalo**

- The highest heaven, where Brahma and Saraswati live with Brahmins; Trikhanda Suggests the three worlds, sky, earth and the subterrain below the ocean;

Airavat

- A mythological white elephant that carries the Hindu God, Indra; Mohiniastra – A weapon that dispels any form of maya in the vicinity; Sudarshan Chakra - A spinning, disk-like super weapon with 108 serrated edges used by the Hindu God, Vishnu; Gada – A mace

SOMAYAGA

Charpati's feat made Lord Indra feel envious and he asked the Guru of all Gods, Bruhaspati, "I do not have the Vaataakarshan Vidya that Charpati possesses. No God knows it either, so what can be done about it? What can be done to acquire that Vidya?" He continued saying, "If I acquire that Vidya my Indra-pad* will be taken away. Accepting Nath's discipleship, suffering hardships and moving from place to place is not something Gods will be able to do. To acquire Sanjeevani Vidya, Kach had been to Shukracharya and he had to face hardships!

Bruhaspati said, "You perform the Somayaga*! Along with all Gods invite the Navnaths for Yajna. Praise them! Honor them so that they are pleased. And then with love and sweetness try to get the Vaataakarshan Vidya from them." Lord Indra took into consideration the other Gods thoughts on it and decided to perform the Somayaga. It was decided to send the first invitation to Macchindranath

They thought, Uparichar Vasu is the father of Macchindranath and so if he gets an invite from him, he will surely come. Lord Indra appealed the Vasu, "You send an invitation to Macchindranath, Gorakshanath and the other Navnaths along with their disciples for attending the Somayaga. Uparichar Vasu went to Badrikaashram where Macchindranath was. Coincidently at that time, Goraksha, Kaanif, Gopichand, Adabanganath and Dharmanath were also present at Badrikaashram. He gave everyone Lord Indra's Somayaga invitation and said, "This is not just an invitation for the ritual but also an appeal for your support in the Somayaga." The Naths felt gratified! It was decided that Macchindranath will gather everyone

First Nath went to Helapattan by plane. He told Mainavati about the invitation for Somayaga of Gods and took her along. Then he went on to pick up the Vatsiddha Naagnath, Bhartari, Revannath and Charpatinath from wherever they were on pilgrimage

Macchindranath had suggested that Somayaga be performed at the Sinhala Island and the Gods agreed to it by asking him to take the initiative. Padmini and Meenanath were also present there. They were also told of the entire plan of action. They took along eighty-four sages of the Nath community. The Yajna started and Lord Indra was sitting for it. Along with the Naths even he was offering sacrifice in the Yajna. On one hand Macchindranath took out time and started teaching Meenanath the Mantra of Astravidya*. Noticing that, Bruhaspati told Lord Indra, "Let Uparichar Vasu host it from here on and you get up

Macchindra is teaching Meenanath the Mantra of Astras. You take the form of a peacock and listen to it secretly. You will get the Vaataakarshan Siddhi." Lord Indra did so! Later while having a conversation, Lord Indra happened to tell Macchindranath about his act. "In this way you'll heard the Mantravidya without our permission and so it will be of no use to any God" saying this he disappointed all Gods. He said, "If the people of the Nath Community are not troubled by Gods only then will it be useful to the Gods." And so the Naths always have the blessings of all Gods

After the Somayaga, Lord Indra stayed on Sahya Mountain for meditation. He got the water of the Manikarnika and poured it at a place from where originated the Indrayani River

The Naths for many years; till the year 1710 did pilgrimages all over, then decided to serve the common man and took Samadhi at various places. Amongst them, Gopichand, Mainavati and Dharmanath went to Heaven, Bhartari stayed in Hades and Goraksha stayed in Badrikaashram

Fruition

The recitation of this chapter will fulfill all the wishes like Paris and Kaamdhenu. And will also get the Sacrosanct of reading the entire manuscript.

***Indra-pa**

- Lord Indra's kingdom and his Kingship;

Somayag

- A sacrifice at which the juice of soma is drunk

Astravidy

- The knowledge of astras (weapons)

Don't miss out!

Visit the website below and you can sign up to receive emails whenever santosh thorat publishes a new book. There's no charge and no obligation.

https://books2read.com/r/B-A-EFKY-MPWJC

BOOKS 2 READ

Connecting independent readers to independent writers.

Did you love *Maha Yogi: An Adventurous and Thrilling Story of Matsyendranath*? Then you should read *The Sacred Journey Within: Unleashing the Power of Celibacy*[1] by santosh thorat!

[2]

The Power of Celibacy: A Guide to Spiritual, Mental, and Physical Well-Being

Celibacy is the practice of abstaining from sexual activity. It can be a powerful tool for spiritual, mental, and physical well-being.

Spiritually, celibacy can help you to connect with your higher power. It can also help you to develop self-discipline and self-control.

Mentally, celibacy can help you to reduce stress, anxiety, and depression. It can also help you to improve your concentration and focus.

---

1. https://books2read.com/u/boqX80

2. https://books2read.com/u/boqX80

Physically, celibacy can help you to improve your overall health and well-being. It can also help you to increase your energy levels and reduce your risk of sexually transmitted diseases.

If you are interested in learning more about the power of celibacy, this book is for you. It provides a comprehensive overview of the benefits of celibacy, as well as practical tips for making it a part of your life.

Here are some of the benefits of celibacy:

Increased spiritual connection

Improved self-discipline and self-control

Reduced stress, anxiety, and depression

Improved concentration and focus

Increased energy levels

Reduced risk of sexually transmitted diseases

If you are ready to experience the power of celibacy, this book is the perfect place to start.The "Power of Celibacy" is a soul-stirring book that delves deep into the life-changing practice of sexual purity and self-control. With the power of words that will move your heart and soul, this book is a powerful guide to the transformative benefits of celibacy, urging you to embark on a journey of self-discovery and spiritual growth.As you delve into the pages of this book, you'll explore the depths of your own being, discovering the true essence of your existence and the power of your innermost desires. With each turn of the page, you'll be inspired to embrace a life of self-discipline, exploring the deeper meaning of celibacy and its power to transform your life in ways you never thought possible.This book is a beacon of hope for those struggling with sexual addiction, providing practical guidance and emotional support to help you find your way to a life of purity and integrity. You'll discover how to harness your sexual energy to fuel your spiritual growth and personal transformation, and how to cultivate healthy relationships that honor and respect your true self.With the "Power of Celibacy," you'll be empowered to take control of your life, harnessing the power of your own inner strength to achieve your goals and dreams. This book is a must-read for anyone seeking a deeper understanding of themselves and the world around them, and a profound reminder of the transformative power of celibacy.

Also by santosh thorat

First Series
Sadhguru Thoughts

Standalone
Indian Yogi: Adventures and Thriller Story
The Sacred Journey Within: Unleashing the Power of Celibacy
Maha Yogi: An Adventurous and Thrilling Story of Matsyendranath
Spiritual Diary: A Diary for Every Spirit
Unlocking the Inner Potential: A Guide to Activating Kechari Mudra
Durga Saptashati: The Sacred Mantras of Goddess Durga
The Barbarik: Enchanted Warrior Story

About the Author

A dedicated spiritual researcher and writer with over 5 years of experience exploring various spiritual traditions, practices, and teachings. With a deep passion for exploring the mysteries of the universe and the nature of consciousness, I have dedicated my career to studying and writing about topics related to spirituality, mindfulness, meditation, and personal growth. Throughout my career, I have gained a reputation for my deep insight, clear writing style, and ability to distill complex spiritual concepts into accessible and practical guidance for readers and audiences. I am passionate about helping others find their own spiritual path and discovering their inner wisdom and truth.

Read more at https://www.goodreads.com/author/list/18209934.Santosh_Thorat.

www.ingramcontent.com/pod-product-compliance
Lightning Source LLC
Chambersburg PA
CBHW071915120726
48001CB00005B/1746